The Rabbi Wore Moccasins

"Ethics is my real love..."

Arthur Gross Schaefer

Arthur Gross Schaefer

The Rabbi Wore Moccasins

Gaon Books

Gaon Books
www.gaonbooks.com

For permissions, group pricing, and other information contact Gaon Books, P.O. Box 23924, Santa Fe, NM 87502 or write (editor@gaonbooks.com). Manufactured in the United States of America.
The paper used in this publication is acid free and meets all ANSI (American National Standards for Information Sciences) standards for archival quality paper. All wood product components used in this book are Sustainable Forest Initiative (SFI) certified.

Library of Congress Cataloging-in-Publication Data

Gross Schaefer, Arthur.
  The rabbi wore moccasins / Arthur Gross Schaefer.
     p. cm.
  ISBN 978-1-935604-41-9 (pbk. : alk. paper) -- ISBN 978-1-935604-42-6 (e-book)
  1. Rabbis--Fiction. 2. Lawyers--Fiction. 3. Legal ethics--Fiction. 4. Indians of North America--Fiction. 5. Casinos--Fiction. I. Title.
  PS3607.R65553R33 2012
  813'.6--dc23
                    2012019368

Special thanks to:
Steve Cook
Paige Blagg
Kathe Segall
Elissa Pociask
Brenda Kirsch
Dr. Richard Seigle
Rose Lighter
Especially my love, Laurie Gross Schaefer

Main Characters

Rabbi Elijah Daniels, Rabbi
Leah, Rabbi Daniels' deceased wife
Ann Gold, Rabbi's secretary
Sue Miller, studying to convert
Blue Star, elder, runs sweat lodge ceremony
Morning Breeze, Fire Keeper
Carol, Blue Star's wife
White Eagle, elder and alleged murderer
Ruth, White Eagle's wife and murder victim
Burt Steel, county inspector
Brenda, housekeeper
Detective Markman, police officer
Jailer
Joy, Ruth's friend
Linda, Ruth's friend
Blossom, Ruth's friend
Tim Hartley, Public Defender
Antchu - Native American tribe
Tom Singer, prison guard
Mike Tall House, casino manager
Rachael, Zac, Adam, Rabbi Daniels' children
Matt, car driver
City - St. Luke's
County - Roseville
Temple Shalom - name of the Rabbi's congregation

Chapter 1
The Murder

Who sheds blood destroys the divine image.
Talmud

"Are the rumors true?" demanded a gritty female voice.

"Don't you ever knock?" Rabbi Elijah Daniels said without looking up. He knew the voice belonged to his secretary, Ann Gold. He took off his seamless bifocal gold-rim glasses and carefully placed them on his roll top desk. It was the end of a long Thursday, filled with unending phone calls, an education committee meeting, hospital visits and lunch with his synagogue president. He was exhausted and finally had some time to prepare the sermon he had to give Friday night. He was looking over his well- worn, blue covered *Hertz Biblical Commentary*. It was old and outdated, but he kept it because it was so familiar. It was presented to him at his bar mitzvah when he dreamed of changing the world and he still used it to help prepare his sermons.

"Are you seriously planning to resign?" Ann asked as she stepped towards his desk.

"I really hate rumors," he said, looking up to gauge Ann's reaction to his next statement, "especially true ones."

She smacked her lips, a stall tactic he knew well, so she could deliver a perfectly timed stinging comment. "What is it? Your wife's death? Or is it those Indians you've been hanging out with?"

"What are you talking about? You are way out of bounds!" Rabbi Daniels responded irately.

"Hey, I'm your secretary. You've been really moody lately. I'm sorry Leah died. That was two years ago. You have three wonderful children, a lot of people who like you, and you continue to walk around depressed. And, you're doing some really curious things. Usually I know who you see, whom you call. I listen through the door. You've been doing a lot of secret meetings and phone calls. Even in the synagogue people are talking! You think a rabbi can hang out with 'Native Americans' and not be noticed? Everyone knows. Some think it's cool, most think it's just strange. Personally, I think it's bizarre."

As if on cue, the phone rang and Ann, showing her frustration, reached over the desk to grab the rabbi's phone. "Hello, this is Temple Shalom, may I help you?" This was one of the few temples that refused to put in an automated answering service because they wanted to keep a friendly tone. Ann was silently listening; then she pushed the red hold button and looked at Rabbi Daniels with a clear look of scorn on her face.

"It's one of your Native American friends," she hissed as she thrust the phone at the rabbi.

The rabbi pushed the hold button. "Hello, this is Rabbi Daniels," using his normal greeting to calm his nerves. Ann could be feisty, but this was odd behavior, even for her.

It took a moment for him to register that the voice on the phone was speaking in a very urgent tone. "Rabbi, this is Blue Star, I'm sorry to bother you, but I don't know who else to call. You've helped us in the past and we need you again!" he continued, his voice rising. "White Eagle's wife was shot. She died. Grandfather White Eagle was arrested as her murderer!"

This did not make sense to the rabbi. He automatically whispered under his breath, *"Baruch Dayan Ha amet."*

Blue Star apparently hadn't noticed and continued talking. "He was taken to the county jail. A Mr. Hartley has been appointed as his public defender. He just called me. He didn't sound hopeful. He didn't seem to care. Would you please call him? Maybe you can do something."

The rabbi was confused and a little annoyed that he was being asked to get involved. Someone he barely knew was dead and the person who was accused of the murder was someone he respected and liked. He looked up noticing that Ann had not moved.

"I'm not a criminal attorney and I really wouldn't be of any help."

"Please, just a phone call," Blue Star pleaded over the phone.

"OK. Are you at Gus' Bar?" the rabbi glanced up to see Ann's disdain. "Give me the number and I'll call back if I get through to Hartley."

As he hung up, he declared, "You can leave now, the show is over."

Ann just smiled. "I heard enough and I'm curious. I can either listen in on my phone or just stay here and listen in on your other phone by the couch. Which do you prefer?"

Rabbi Daniels looked at this somewhat short-statured, yet robust and striking, brunette in her early 50s. He knew that she took long hikes and probably was in better shape than he although he was five years younger. She was well entrenched when he became the rabbi of this small California synagogue almost a year ago. She knew everyone and kept her ear to the gossip in the air that seemed to constantly blow through the temple like a summer breeze rippling through a field of wheat. He had thought of getting a younger secretary who would help change the image of the synagogue and who, he presumed, would be more computer savvy. He also did not appreciate her strong opinions, which she always seemed to feel she had a right to share with him whenever she wanted. However, he had learned quickly that her computer skills were quite formidable and her knowledge of the temple's culture was invaluable-so much for his ageism. She embodied the temple's spirit and was a walking historian of the temple's lore. And this knowledge had saved him more than once. She could tell him the personal history of almost every temple member. She knew who was upset with whom and how best to approach the various donors when the temple was in need of money, which it generally was.

He remembered one incident soon after he had arrived when he was about to begin the bar mitzvah service for Richard Friedman. Ann had rushed into his study and literally pulled him from his pre-service meeting by the arm into the hallway. How dare she invade his study, he had thought at the time. He had felt embarrassed and thought she was rude, not to mention insubordinate. However, before the rabbi could share his righteous indignation, she cautioned, "I need to warn you. Richard's father is here."

He had blurted out in an angry tone, "What do you mean? Of course the father is here!"

"No, you don't understand. You thought that the man with Mrs. Friedman was Richard's father. He isn't; he's her long time boyfriend," Ann continued. "The tall angry man leaning on the gift shop counter, wearing the blue blazer, that is Bill Sawyer, Richard's biological father. He wasn't invited.

I don't think they thought he would come and I am guessing you weren't told anything," she asserted in a triumphant tone.

The rabbi nodded his head in agreement. She was right and he was at a loss. He really didn't know how to deal with the situation.

"They are so stupid!" Ann added this last comment in a tone suggestive of a parent scolding a young child for lying about brushing their teeth when the toothbrush remained perfectly dry. "I know Bill," she continued. "If he doesn't get a role, play the part of father, he'll be likely to feel deeply hurt and make a scene." She now took the opportunity to give the rabbi her unsolicited advice, "I'd go up and tell Mrs. Friedman that since her ex-husband has arrived, it is important to keep the service focused on the bar mitzvah and not on any history between the parents. You want her permission to include the father in the service." Well, that is exactly what he did and, although Mrs. Friedman was not so happy with the change of events, everyone got along, at least during the service and the reception.

The rabbi shuddered to think what could have happened with the disgruntled father had Ann not been there to preempt the problem. Since he had grown to respect and trust her opinion and loyalty, he grudgingly had to admit that he considered her a confidant, someone he could trust. He also liked her. "Okay, okay, stay here and listen. But, do try to not give me those looks," said Rabbi Daniels.

"What 'looks?'" said Ann as she feigned an innocent countenance.

Rabbi Daniels dialed the number given to him by Blue Star. He was surprised when it was picked up after the first ring. "Yeah, this is Tim Hartley."

The rabbi, although he had been a lawyer, didn't practice long enough to become totally confident. He never got the knack of speaking quickly on his feet, so he stammered, "This is Rabbi...I mean this is Rabbi Daniels. I'm calling about White Eagle."

"Oh yeah. I was told you'd be calling. I got White Eagle's permission to talk with you. What do you want to know?"

The rabbi couldn't tell much except the man seemed busy and distracted. He had once thought of becoming a public defender or a legal aid attorney, helping those whose right to legal protection had been pushed aside. But, when he had interned at a legal aid office in Boston while in law school, he had become staggered by the lack of appreciation he felt from the clients. He expected, naively at the time, to be profusely thanked for his altruism. In reality, he did not feel respected; he primarily experienced their anger, sometimes directed at him. He felt that he was simply being viewed as just part of the system that his few beleaguered clients believed was responsible for crushing their spirit. He knew he couldn't exist in that environment of rage that lacked gratitude and he absently wondered if he felt he was in a similar environment at the synagogue. Rabbi Daniels surprised himself when he said, "Well, I'm not a criminal attorney and I'm not really sure why I'm calling. I'm not sure I can help."

"Look Rabbi, I'm not sure anyone can help. Perhaps you can pray for a miracle. This seems like a rather open and shut domestic squabble that turned ugly." He listed the evidence as if he were reading a grocery list. "White Eagle's finger prints were on the gun, there was gun powder residue on his right hand, he acknowledged owning the gun, he had been angry at his wife, he was drunk, and he openly admitted to killing her both in his call to 911 and when the police and paramedics arrived," said Hartley.

The rabbi was stunned. "But, why? Why did he kill her?"

"Apparently, she was working at the casino on the reservation and he didn't like it. Got drunk and shot at her several times. One of the bullets found its mark."

"What do you plan to do?" The rabbi asked in a shaky but resigned voice. He had known a few public defenders; one from his graduating class had even chosen this path and he had heard she was quite happy. How had she learned to cope and even thrive in such an environment? What had she learned which he had not? Were his expectations unrealistic or was his skin just too thin to be a good public defender or rabbi? Generally, he believed public defenders were good lawyers. And, to be honest with himself, he was somewhat envious that they knew how to work the legal system in spite of being overworked and under appreciated, they did very credible jobs.

"Unless you have some brilliant ideas, I can't think of any defense beyond the basic diminished capacity owing to his being drunk. Due to his age, I doubt if the DA will ask for the death penalty or could even prove special circumstances. Probably the best bet is some type of plea bargain."

The rabbi was silent for a long moment. As if talking to himself he acknowledged, "Jail time would probably kill him. But," he paused and then as if talking to himself again said, "perhaps there is a possible defense."

The rabbi was taken aback when the public defender's demeanor suddenly changed. "Are you kidding? This guy confesses, there is no Miranda problem, all the physical evidence links him to the murder - and you think you have a defense. Hey, I know you're a rabbi and a lawyer. Are you a magician too?"

The rabbi was caught off guard and retreated. "Perhaps I'm too hasty. I'm no criminal attorney. Let me think about this and get back to you if I think I really have something."

Hartley was not one to be put off so easily. "Look, you may have good intentions. But this guy's life has been put in my hands. If you have any crazy ideas that just may work, you should tell me now."

The rabbi had forgotten that Ann was in the room listening to the conversation. But now he could feel her eyes boring into him. "Listen, let me think about this and we'll talk later." With that he hastily hung up the phone.

Ann slowly put down the phone, but her eyes had not left the rabbi's face. Ann was like a vigilant gopher with her head straight up, not moving. "Here is a public defender that works defending criminals all the time and he has no trick up his sleeve. Here you are, a congregational rabbi, an ex-lawyer, and you have a defense. Don't tell me you don't have one and don't tell me you're not sure because you're not a criminal attorney. Don't give me that bull."

The rabbi stood up and began pacing. "Ann, I only practiced law for a short time. I never became competent and sometimes I feel like I never gave law a chance. Perhaps I was too scared and didn't think I could compete successfully. I often wondered if my decision to leave the practice of law and become a rabbi was an escape."

Ann reflected on this admission for only a moment, "Good try. I'm sure you were scared. But, we both know that being a rabbi is no easy or safe job. If you left law for the 'safety' of the rabbinate, I think you made a bad decision. Look, I don't know what's wrong with you or what you're looking for, but, for right now, don't try to escape; you have something up your sleeve, what is it?"

He had stopped pacing while Ann was talking but now resumed his back and forth movement. "There is a legal concept called diminished capacity. Remember the Twinkie defense in San Francisco when the man who killed the city's mayor got off because his attorney argued that he had a sugar high?"

"Diminished capacity? You are going to argue that your Indian friend was so drunk that he lacked the ability to know what he was doing? From what I heard from your conversation with this Hartley, he didn't think much of that idea."

He sat back down on his brown antique captain's chair in front of his weathered desk. He loved this old desk; he brought it with him from his former law practice. He liked how the papers streamed out of various crevasses and reminded him of the prayers and notes that he had seen at the Western Wall in Jerusalem.

"No, that's not it. Now, I haven't fully formed this. Remember, I just thought of it. So bear with me. Before I came here, I did some work in the area of sexual misconduct by rabbis."

"Wait a second!" Now Ann was startled. "I've heard a lot about priests and ministers having sexual issues with congregants. Do you mean to tell me that rabbis...?"

The rabbi stopped pacing and shook his head. "The numbers aren't high. But the psychological currents are strong and rabbis can get dragged out of their depths if not careful. We talk a lot about 'transference' in this work, the trust that people automatically give to their clergy. They believe that the actions of their clergy are proper and in the best interest of the congregant and the community."

Ann's impatience was showing, "But what does this have to do with a defense for White Eagle killing his wife?"

The rabbi was suddenly excited, like a football coach explaining a touchdown play to his team. "Here's how I would do it. Jury selection is one of the most important parts of a trial. I'd use my challenges strategically and maneuver the jury to be made up of as many church-going individuals as possible who like their ministers. My hope, or prayer if you wish, would be to bring witness after witness so that these jurors would begin viewing White Eagle as a deeply holy man, a clergyman, with deep and traditional values, who had worked to save his community and wanted to protect it."

"You can really control what type of people get onto a jury in such a specific way?" Ann asked.

13

"Today we have jury consultants and even therapists that advise lawyers who they should pick for the jury. You've seen those films about trying to control a jury," the Rabbi continued; he was on a roll and didn't want to stop. "Once they see him as a religious and pious individual, I would talk about the casino. Like Professor Hill in the Music Man, I would parade evidence of the damning nature of gambling on the moral fabric of the community and its youth before that religious jury. Next, I would describe White Eagle's valiant yet futile effort to protect his community by his strong opposition to the building of the casino. They would feel his pain and frustration at losing this moral battle for the souls of the tribe's children."

Ann couldn't stop herself from interrupting, "You sound like a born again preacher. But how do you know all this?"

Rabbi Daniels ignored her as he continued, "and then there would be the climax." The Rabbi's hand shot up. "The betrayal!" He turned and faced Ann, his brown eyes burning into hers. "His wife, who should have stood with him, brazenly flaunted his authority and his public position as a spiritual leader. She goes to work at the very institution, which he had fought so hard to stop, the evil casino. This public humiliation is too much - he loses control and kills her in a fit of self righteous rage against all the evil that is stealing the souls of his community's children."

The rabbi stopped. "All we need is one juror who would have sympathy for him. It could work. I think it could actually work." He was now silent, his body spent.

Ann was silent just for a moment, her teeth clenched, her face turning red, and then she exploded. "You are going to try to get him off by blaming his wife! We always blame the victim. If it's rape, it's the woman's fault for leading a man on. If she's harassed in the workplace, then she shouldn't have worn such tight-fitting clothing." She paused for emphasis and in a patronizing tone concluded, "I presume you would ideally want a lot of male chauvinist pigs on the jury as well?"

The rabbi's hands shot up as if fending off arrows. "Take a deep breath. Relax. Now you're supposed to ask me a question."

Still with a sharp edge to her voice, "What question?"

"Why didn't I tell the public defender this theory?" Rabbi Daniels said softly, raising his eyebrows.

Ann's mood swings were legendary. Her posture changed, becoming more relaxed. Now her face leisurely morphed into a grin. She giggled. "Wouldn't you have achieved the legal heights by getting a guilty man off? Just think of the headlines: 'Rabbi uses unique defense to gain an acquittal of confessed murderer.' You'd be famous and on all those talk shows. And, since you apparently don't want to be a rabbi anymore"-- Ann couldn't resist a twist of the knife -- "you could become a wealthy defense attorney. So, why didn't you tell him about your defense theory?"

The rabbi absentmindedly began pulling and rubbing his ear. "It did cross my mind that this would be a highly publicized case. And, I did picture myself cross-examining witnesses and talking to the press. It would have all been very exciting. My *yetzer* was tempted."

"Your what?"

"Within every person there are inclinations to do good things and evil things. Not exactly evil; rather, things that we do to satisfy our ego. And my ego was soaring when I thought about being involved." His hands fell at his side.

"So what stopped you?" Ann asked.

"You know I run this monthly study group for judges and lawyers. So, I've taught about the Jewish tradition and being an ethical attorney. There are two basic criteria as to whether or not one should take a case. First, do I believe in the integrity of the individual? Here, the answer is yes. I like and trust White Eagle. Second, do I believe in the case I'll be making? You asked how I knew all that I was saying. Well, I know some things here and there. And, some I made up. While I think my defense is ingenious, if I must say so myself, I'm guessing there is a good chance I can find witnesses and evidence to make this case. But, I don't want to make this case. I don't want clergy, elders or anyone thinking that they could be exempt from responsibility because they could not control their own passions."

He continued, "Our tradition asks who is strong? One is strong who can control their passion." He was silent. His mind drifted off.

"Your reasoning sounds good," Ann ventured, "but also a little self serving. Why not see if your theory is really worth anything. After all, you told me that you really didn't practice all that much and not in criminal law. There are several lawyers in the congregation. Run your idea past one of them."

"You may be cute, but you are a real killjoy. I'm sorry I even told you," Rabbi Daniels exclaimed with some irritation that turned into brooding.

"If your idea is sound, will you ever tell the public defender or will you just let White Eagle go to jail?"

Rabbi Daniels remained brooding. He had to acknowledge that Ann was somewhat right. He was a little afraid to expose himself to the public defender. He thought his idea was good, but he wasn't sure. He didn't want to be laughed at, not in front of Ann. He had always been a little afraid to take stands. He wished he were more certain of himself and what he was doing as a lawyer and, to be honest, as a rabbi.

"By the way, you whispered some Hebrew words when you learned that White Eagle's wife had been killed. What did you say?"

The Rabbi was awakened by Ann's question.

"*Baruch Dayan Ha amet* - Blessed is the G-d of truth. It's the traditional phrase which one says upon hearing of a death."

"What a strange thing to say," Ann muttered. "I've not heard you say it before."

"I do it quietly, privately. It is intended to be strange, even shocking. At the moment of loss when there is great pain and probably great anger, our tradition asks one to do the impossible. We make a statement that reaffirms the belief in a just G-d. For me, it demands that I see death as I see life, both miracles of the divine."

Ann was thinking about this answer in relation to the death of her husband and the rage she had felt about being cheated out of so much left for them to share, but she had another set of questions. "Who is White Eagle? How did you meet him? And why would a well respected rabbi begin spending so much time with Indians?"

Rabbi Daniels noticed that the sun was leaving a beautiful sunset as it escaped behind the mountains, filling the sky with yellows, reds, blues and purples. "How much time do you have?"

Chapter 2
The Convert

All beginnings are hard.
Mikilta to Exodus, 19.5

The rabbi called his housekeeper, Brenda. "Hey, is it okay if I'm home late tonight? I know...I know. I promised to help Zac with his East Timor report. However, I just got a call about someone I know who has been arrested for killing his wife. I'm talking with my assistant... Yes, I can't believe it...Tell Zac I'll help tomorrow night...Will you be okay with the kids? Thanks." Rabbi Daniels hung up the phone and Ann returned with two glasses and a bottle of white Westhoffner Bergkloster. "This bottle was left from the Bergin's wedding last night. I don't think they'll miss it." She had already uncorked it and poured a large glass for the rabbi and herself. She sat down in the soft leather chair across from Rabbi Daniels. "OK, begin."

"My connection to the Antchu started by someone who wanted to convert. You know her, it was Sue. Remember when she came here for the first time? She was wearing a tie-dyed shirt, a blue bandana, a white skirt and leather sandals."

"I'm Sue Miller," a tall blond-haired woman declared, holding out her hand self-assuredly. As the rabbi stood and began to move from his desk towards her, the blood seemed to drain from her face as she suddenly struggled to take a step backwards, simultaneously jerking her hands behind her back, almost losing her balance.

"I'm sorry. I'm so sorry. I know that I shouldn't shake a rabbi's hand. I'm just so new to this whole thing. And I wanted to do it right. Sorry." This last comment was made as the first trickle of tears began to fall from her eyes. The rabbi was startled that the seemingly confident woman who had just entered his office had been reduced to tears without him saying or doing anything. He wondered what Ann was thinking in the outer office. He knew she loved to listen through the open door of his study. He also knew that Ann was very good at keeping whatever she heard confidential. Even though he trusted Ann, he didn't want to tempt her. He gently closed the door, offered his guest a box of Kleenex and asked her to "please sit down."

18

"Please," he informed in his best soothing voice, "you did nothing wrong and I will gladly shake your hand in just a moment. You were right to be careful and there are some rabbis who don't shake a woman's hand for a variety of reasons. Generally, it is because they don't know if it is her menstrual period and whether she is ritually clean or not. To avoid any possible mistake, they just refrain from contact with most women. I don't believe that women are impure during their menstrual cycle when their bodies are performing purely natural functions. I also don't like the idea that women can be viewed as impure, even if it's for a relatively short period of time."

The rabbi knew he was giving a little bit of a longer explanation than was needed; he just wanted to keep talking until he felt that she had regained her composure. As the tears stopped and the color returned to her face, he was sufficiently confident to continue.

"Let's start again." With this utterance, he held out his hand and took a step towards Sue. "My name is Rabbi Daniels and it's a pleasure to meet you, Sue Miller. How can I help?"

As the rabbi approached and asked his question, Sue had carefully stood up straight, grasped the rabbi's hand with a surprisingly strong grip, and blurted, "I want to become Jewish."

The rabbi's self-absorbed thoughts of sadness had temporarily vanished as he was energized by the intensity of the visit. Prior to her arrival, he had once again been thinking about his decision to be a congregational rabbi. He realized that he was doing this more often lately and it was beginning to affect his mood. He invited Sue to sit down and he took a seat in a worn leather armchair and asked simply, "Why? Why do you want to become Jewish?"

"I'm a deeply spiritual person," she stated, staring intently into the rabbi's eyes. It was as if she could no longer contain her pent-up emotions. In a rush of excitement she continued, "I've studied many religions over the years. When I studied Judaism, it touched my mind and my heart." She had gained enough composure to say these last words slowly and she gently raised her hand and patted her chest. "It is such an awesome religion. It's so practical and spiritual at the same time. I believe that my soul is Jewish. And, I want to be with my people."

The rabbi smiled deeply. He had been surprised at the amount of people who had come into his study who had wanted to convert to Judaism. He had assumed most people looking for a new religious path would pick an exotic eastern religion or some more popular tradition. He certainly never thought they would pick a religion, which had been so marginalized and maligned. He truly loved Judaism and saw it -- what was the word Sue used? -- yes, as a truly "awesome religion." He felt uplifted that someone raised outside the tradition was willing to become part of his people.

The rabbi wanted to warn her with the obvious. "Sue, I am so happy with what you have told me. However, you do know that not everyone likes Jews. Our history of persecution is very real." He remembered the time he was beaten up as a child by a group of kids calling him a "Christ killer." He didn't know that Christ meant Jesus; he only saw the hatred in their eyes. He continued his thoughts: "And, I don't believe that there is only one path to G-d. G-d is not Jewish, or Christian, or Catholic, or Islamic, or Buddhist. I honor those who use their religion to bring out humanity, compassion, and love in this all too often hate-filled world. We Jews don't see our mission to convert people. We are not out to 'save' people, rather we are out to partner with other good people to help bring about a better world."

He was angry and a little bitter about all the religious groups that had tried to get Jews to convert over the centuries, using whatever means they had at their disposal from threats to torture. Now, it was done in a more subtle and invidious fashion with slick brochures and pitches that one could be Jewish and believe in Jesus at the same time. Why couldn't they leave his people alone?

Instead, all he revealed to Sue was, "So, you don't have to become Jewish. Be the best Christian you can be." The rabbi couldn't tell what religion Sue was but his guess was that she was a Christian. Whatever religion she was, he didn't want her considering Judaism without making sure that her own religion wasn't right for her. Moreover, he was saying these words as part of the ancient tradition to dissuade converts to better determine their level of seriousness and capacity for thoughtful reflection. Her manner of dress, which hearkened back to the 60s, made the rabbi feel a little uncomfortable and brought up concerns about her mental stability. Nevertheless, he was also becoming a little intrigued. Sue seemed to be a very contemplative and thoughtful person. If she did decide to begin the process of conversion, he expected it to be a very interesting journey for both of them. He had long since learned that often the teacher learns more from the student.

Rabbi Daniels cautioned, "I want you to think a little more about your decision. If you do want to continue, it is not merely a matter of saying some magic words. Rather, it is a process of study, reading, and thinking. And, it will take some time." He looked carefully at Sue to measure her response.

Sue looked at the rabbi, holding his eyes, and answered, "I knew you would try to dissuade me. Remember, I've read a lot about Judaism. I love that too about your tradition. You're not out to impose your views on others. So, the answer is yes, I will come back. The only question for you is when."

As Rabbi Daniels got up to walk to his desk, he picked up a calendar book and went over to his computer. Ann called through the door, as if it had not been closed to exclude her, and as if she knew that this was a safe time to interrupt.

"You've gotten several calls. I've got one on hold, which you should take. It's from the chaplain at the hospital about a sick Christian kid. She needs your advice."

The rabbi quickly smiled in an apologetic way to Sue and picked up the phone.

Sue could see the Rabbi simultaneously talking on a phone crammed against his left ear, typing notes into a computer with one hand, and flipping through a desk calendar with the other. Even with this multitasking, his voice was calm as he responded to his caller, "Yes, I understand, this is most unusual, and I'll be able to be at the hospital around 3:00 this afternoon."

When he hung up, he looked at Sue. His blue and yellow striped tie on his nicely pressed blue dress shirt did not hide the fact that he was troubled and looked tired. The rabbi confided, "There is a young boy who collapsed some time ago and has been in a coma. He has been on a respirator and the doctors believe he is brain dead. The parents are considering taking him off. The chaplain thought they would want to talk with me."

The rabbi paused, his gaze caught by a red tail hawk flying high above the canyon below his office, and continued, "I feel so sorry for the boy and for the parents. There is an old strange Jewish blessing, 'May you die, may your children die, may your grandchildren die.'"

Sue couldn't help saying, "I don't get it. What a depressing blessing."

The rabbi jerked his head when he saw Sue as if he were surprised that he was not alone. He recovered quickly and with a melancholy smile he answered, "Parents see themselves growing old surrounded by their children and grandchildren. They presume that they will die first and then their children. When a child dies before a parent, it is devastating. So this is a blessing about the natural order and that a parent will not have to bury their child."

Sue was silent for a moment, nodded her head and then asked, "I also don't understand why they would want to talk to you? The boy is not Jewish. Wouldn't they want to talk with their priest or minister?"

The rabbi had moved to his desk when the phone call came. He was sitting now in the brown captain's chair in front of his desk. He put on his glasses to better see the computer screen and then turned to face Sue. "There are some clergy who believe they have all the answers and would never dream of asking someone from another faith for help. We have an old saying from our oldest code called the Mishnah put together around the year 200 CE."

Sue again could not help herself from interrupting. "I've read a lot about rabbis and their sayings. Do you really have one for everything?"

The rabbi's smile was now more genuine, although he still did appear tired. "Well, I'm not sure about everything, but, this is one of my favorites. The saying goes 'Who is wise, one who learns from all people.' The chaplain has heard me do presentations on end- of- life decisions. I work in the area of bioethics. Certainly I come from a Jewish perspective and share those views openly. I happen to think that our perspective is both ancient and quite modern at the same time. But, I also believe in the individual's right to choose based on their values and informed by the wisdom of the generations. The Jewish tradition is quite developed and does have a lot to offer in areas of bioethics."

"When you meet with the parents, what will you tell them?"

The rabbi now broke into a hearty chuckle. "Don't confuse me with the all-knowing type who always has the answers. I'm not so wise and neither are the Jewish sources. There are different opinions and even conflicting views. Yes, there are trends. Sometimes traditional Jews see a different trend as more controlling than I would."

He walked over to a black vertical filing cabinet behind his desk, opened up the second drawer from the top and pulled out a thick manila envelope. He continued talking as he selected a few rather worn sheets. "I will take some of our traditional sources and study these with the parents. I want to calm them down and then allow them to hear the wisdom from our ancestors. They will hear the voices of the rabbis from the early centuries, Middle Ages, and contemporary times debating end- of- life issues. I'll ask them to share what they are hearing and what they are learning. Then, I will ask them to combine this with their own values and listen to their hearts. I will not tell them anything, I will only help them to listen. The final decision will be theirs and they need to own their responsibility for the decision they will be making. At the same time, I'll be standing with them as well as will all the previous generations who have had to make similar decisions. They need to know that they are not alone.

"Oh, I'm sorry," Rabbi Daniels offered hurriedly. "You wanted an appointment with me." Then he caught himself and looked up from his computer back into Sue's eyes. "The step you are considering is very serious. Are you sure you want to come back?"

"Not only am I sure that I want to come back, I'm sure I want you as my rabbi. And, I'm worried about you." This last comment caught the rabbi by surprise. Sue continued, "You can tell that I'm one of those that don't keep their emotions in." Rabbi Daniels nodded and waited for her next comment. "Often healers help everyone else but themselves. Well, I'm telling you that you look stressed and sad. I don't know what's going on, but you need some serious time off."

Rabbi Daniels' right hand absentmindedly stroked his formerly black beard that was following the seasons as shades of winter white were encroaching. He slid open the top right drawer and removed a yellow sheet of legal size paper. He picked up the narrow gold colored wire rim glasses on a pile of papers and placed them on his face. He peered at the sheet he held, and without looking up he said, "Let me read you something I wrote."

There are only questions
Why do we choose to sleep through so many beautiful sunrises?
When did we decide that watching television is more interesting, than
    the night sky?
Who told us that collecting things is more important than appreciating
    what freely surrounds us?
Why do we fear death when we know that all dies?

Yet we choose to believe
If we have faith, we can live with the questions
If we trust there is a purpose, we feel imbued with meaning
If we have conviction, then there is passion in our lives
If we find others, we feel reassured

And, there is G-d
G-d gives our lives meaning
G-d provides us with understanding
G-d nourishes our soul
G-d is our partner in the act of creation

Nevertheless, the questions remain
Am I on a spiritual path or merely walking down a path?
Am I able to live with the questions or in reality am I too busy with
    the answers?
Am I really able to pray or am I just saying words?

Am I seeking G-d or am I pretending?

And I remain--- questioning and, alone.

Sue broke the silence. She had closed her eyes while the rabbi read and now opened them to gaze at him. "I've heard your sermons and I've read the types of readings you select. I've never heard you say anything like this. Are you lonely?"

Perhaps because he was tired, he just needed to talk. "I didn't become a rabbi until I was already a lawyer. And, I didn't become a rabbi to serve a congregation. Even though I have achieved the appearance of a 'successful' lifestyle, how I live my daily life leaves me somewhat empty. Although I didn't know it, I have always wanted to go beyond myself and feel connected to the sand, the stars, and the trees. I want to feel the connection to nature and be fully engaged in life. I did not want to feel alone."

Raising his head and looking out the window at the gray green oak trees that framed the distant bluish mountains for over a hundred years, he said, "Being a rabbi nowadays is more like a vending machine. Congregants want me to provide for them. If it's a wedding, I am to be joyous. At a funeral, I am to be appropriately mournful. If a member is thinking of leaving, I must find or do something to make sure they stay. My sermons are to be fun, entertaining, and meaningful. But if I really challenge them to change their lives, all hell breaks loose. It's like we have an agreement-I won't push the congregation to do anything it doesn't want to do and I can say and do pretty much what I want."

Rabbi Daniels stood up. "It's a good arrangement for keeping things steady and safe. It's a terrible arrangement if we really believe that G-d wants us to do something serious with our lives." And then, as an afterthought, "Carrying everyone's burden of being the official Jew is very hard and lonely."

Sue had been listening and now she spoke. "You need to do something different and I have an idea. Have you ever gone to a Native American sweat?"

"What?" The rabbi was startled. What was she talking about? He had clearly shared too much, made himself too vulnerable. What was he doing letting down his guard like this? Was he still that miserable from losing Leah to a damned car accident? He could only answer, "No."

"Well, I've told you that I've studied a lot of religions and I find a sweat to be quite relaxing and cleansing. And, I'm going to one this Sunday. You should come with me."

The rabbi looked out the window back at the hawk which seemed to be flying lower, closer to the synagogue, closer to the rabbi's study, and he opened up the computer program to look at his calendar for Sunday. Could a well-respected congregational Rabbi even consider going to a sweat lodge, let alone actually do it, he pondered? Could he, a widower, go with a single woman who was a potential convert? Who was also attractive? Would anyone know? What the heck, he thought. What harm would it do to do something different? Surprisingly, this Sunday was relatively free after he told a morning story to the summer camp kids at the synagogue. Usually his Sundays were packed with teaching, doing a ritual such as a baby naming or home dedication, or attending some community function as the Jewish representative. Without fully realizing why or the possible consequences, he asked, "I'll be free after 10am, does that work?"

Sue smiled. "I'll pick you up at your home at 10:30. Dress comfortably, perhaps in jeans. Bring a towel, a pair of shorts to change into and an extra shirt."

The rabbi was typing the information into his computer. "And what time will we be back?"

Still smiling, Sue replied, "You will learn about time from a Native American point of view. You'll be back when you get back."

Chapter 3
The Sweat

G-d was in this place and I did not know it.
Genesis

nn noticed that it was dinner time and she was hungry. She could also sense that the rabbi wanted to tell more of his story, "Will Brenda be okay with the kids if you're not home for dinner?"

"I think she'll be fine. She knows I'll probably be home late. But I really don't want to go out."

"Well, we don't have to. The Bergin's left us a lot more than just some wine from their party. There is great cold salmon with a zesty dill sauce, green salad, and asparagus with a lemon sauce. I had some for lunch and there is a lot more. I wouldn't mind a second helping. Are you enticed?" Ann asked like an experienced waiter at a fine restaurant.

They got up, picked up their used glasses along with the empty wine bottle and proceeded down the hall to the large kitchen. Usually the synagogue was busy with meetings or classes. He was happy that this was not one of those nights. It was still, which was exactly the right mood for him.

Rabbi Daniels sat on a stool and watched Ann opening cabinets and the refrigerator. She finally returned with two plates piled high with fish, salad and vegetables. But, she wasn't finished; she brought out another bottle of wine. "If I didn't know better, I'd say you're trying to seduce me," the rabbi wryly quipped.

"Don't flatter yourself," Ann answered quickly. "You're not my type and you're not my age. You're not mature enough." Ann felt a little blush coming over her. "Before you go on with your story, tell me more about why you're so damned depressed. It's not just Sue who has noticed, a lot of other people are concerned as well."

Why was he so sad? That was a good question, the rabbi asked himself. It was such a strange and ominous feeling. But he was deeply gloomy and he knew it. He had been a lawyer and a university professor; now he was in a new career. He didn't think anyone noticed, or worse, felt, his depression. He presumed that everyone saw him as always being upbeat and positive. When he used to call one of his ex-girlfriends at work and she would hear his voice, she would say loudly for all to hear, "It's Mr. Sunshine on the phone." He wondered where "Mr. Sunshine" was now. Certainly he was no longer a young man, as his sore muscles often proved after he played a game of tennis. He could still keep his own most of the time, but his Achilles tendon always hurt. It was just a few years ago that he tore this tendon and was told that he would always have to be a little careful. Still, he was a healthy six foot one inch man who had once loved deeply. For the last few weeks he could not shake the persistent feeling that something was profoundly wrong. And it wasn't just that he was a widower, which was such an awful term. That was terrible, but there was also something else. It was simply that he was wrong; he was in the wrong place doing the wrong thing. He expressed these feelings to Ann while he ate the leftover salmon. He felt like he was making a confession to a priest. If he expected her sympathy, he didn't get much.

"Yes, you lost someone you loved and that is hard. So did I. But, you've only been here for a year and you're already giving up. You think you'll be happier going back to law or teaching? I think there is too much self-pity here. Anyway, the food is good, the wine is great, go on with the story."

He didn't like her rather demanding attitude and seemingly compassionless reaction to this baring of his soul. On the other hand, maybe she had a point. Maybe there was too much self-pity. He had great children that too often tried his patience, and a position of respect and honor. He knew that he should be happy and he was certain that he wasn't. He didn't feel successful as a rabbi or a father, and to be painfully truthful, as a former husband. He hated the word "widower." He was always busy doing a lot of things for a lot of people and never seemed to have had enough time for his children or for Leah. And now she was gone.

He took another fork full of salmon, dipped it in the dill sauce and began.

It was 10:30 on the hot, windless, August morning. He had just told one of his "famous" children's stories to the camp kids and was now waiting for Sue. He loved making up stories for the temple's children and for his own. Last night was a bar mitzvah party at which he stayed at much longer than normal. He usually avoided staying at bar mitzvah parties as it took away any private time for the kids. He liked to have the family go to a movie or take a walk along the beach. He also remembered his walks with Leah when she talked about her art and her various projects. He didn't know where she got the inspiration to create her amazing pieces.

Yet, it also frustrated him that her art and clients had taken so much of her time and spirit. He missed her and still would talk with her at night. She had an inner knowledge and insight that would always make him stand in awe of her creations. He knew that as G-d had to create to express G-d's spirit, Leah had to create as well. And, he had encouraged her. It was on one of her visits to a congregation in San Diego that she had been killed. He guessed that she would have encouraged him to move on, to begin dating, to try new things.

He wondered what he was doing going to a sweat lodge on a Sunday morning. He finally had a day off and he could go see a movie, one of his favorite things to do when he had time. His thoughts were interrupted when Sue's old yellow Chevy station wagon arrived. There was no mistaking her car with its loose muffler announcing its arrival.

With a bag containing a pair of shorts, a towel and a change of shirt, the Rabbi greeted Sue with a question. "Do you think we should take my car?" Sue's station wagon had been bright yellow at least a generation in the past. The interior, the rabbi thought, will provide some future archaeologist with abundant information about our society-discarded Diet Coke cans, abandoned bags of Bell Brand chips, and fatigued copies of People magazine. Some were so old that he didn't even know whose picture adorned the drab

28

and ragged covers. The taped seats resembled encased mummies. And the engine did not inspire confidence due to its loose muffler that had let all those within earshot know this was a car in need of major repair. His confidence about the car and the trip was certainly shaken.

"Ye of little faith," was her joyful response. "Get in and pray."

It was over a three-hour drive from St. Luke's, where the rabbi lived and worked, to where the sweat was held. The sun had already lifted its head high above the purplish mountains of the Pacific coast. He looked out the window as the rays of the yellow sun flew across blue-black ocean swells frosted with foam. And then in amazement and awe he spotted the black dorsal fin of a bottle nosed dolphin surfing one of the waves.

"You know, Sue, in the Jewish tradition nature is never to be taken for granted. It is seen as an act of creation by G-d who allows the sun to rise, animals to exist and a new day of wonder to begin. When one sees a beautiful creation, one says a prayer thanking G-d for the act of creation." That morning the rabbi felt free and particularly thankful-excited while a bit apprehensive. He chanted a blessing in Hebrew and translated for Sue's benefit, "Blessed are You, Ruler of the universe, who is the Creator of all things."

Ann had been silent for longer than usual. "We do have a lot of blessings, come to think of it."

"Well, I had one teacher in rabbinic school who proudly would tell us that our tradition had a blessing for every major event. There were blessings for seeing the ocean for the first time, viewing a rainbow, and even being in the presence of a scholar. I certainly think you should learn that prayer and use it in my presence," the rabbi jokingly added.

"However, I had a woman friend who would challenge him. She used to say that the tradition had a blessing for all events that were relevant to males. She then pointed out that there were no traditional prayers for a miscarriage, menopause, or even when a young girl began her menstrual cycle."

"She's right," declared Ann.

"Yes, she is," agreed Rabbi Daniels.

"So, what have you done about it?" challenged Ann.

"Hey, why always put things on me? For your information, my woman friend is now a very well known rabbi for a major congregation. And, she and others have created prayers and rituals especially for these events. And, I have used many of them. So, am I still on your good guy list?"

"Yes. Now continue the story," Ann demanded with mock authority.

Both were silent, still hearing the blessing in their minds and enjoying the journey. All too soon they turned off the coastal highway and began weaving over the citadel of mountains with their layers of reddish-green chaparral and a variety of green pine and grayish oak trees, with a few large yellow leafy sycamores near the creek beds. They continued the snake-like trek up the back of the seemingly endless mountain. The rabbi was now becoming a little tired of the drive and had a growing fear that Sue's car was about to expire. He had not seen a house or a car for that matter for a considerable amount of time. He was rather sure that Sue did not belong to the AAA. What would happen when they broke down? How would he get back to his home? Suddenly, he was not feeling so well.

The rabbi felt as if he was stuck in the old nursery rhyme about a little bear that climbs to the top of the mountain to only find another mountain. Finally they reached the crest, which still contained remnants of blackened snow. After a few minutes, the pine trees were left behind and replaced with a seeming monochromatic painting of browns, beiges, and tans. The sky was a brilliant, deep, and endless blue. The rabbi had not been in the desert for a long time and always thought that the blue over the ocean was bright. Yet now it was clear that this was a more intense blue than he had seen in a long time, perhaps even since he had been a rabbinic student climbing Mt. Sinai, and the Israeli sky almost overpowered his eyes. Beyond the browns, there were blues, purples, greens, and reds. This apparently dead land was full of live jackrabbits whose ears were bigger than their bodies and red tail hawks whose grace was the envy of ballerinas. Certainly there were no pine trees here, which was his usual boyhood reference to being in nature. But there was beauty and life in the desert.

The rabbi broke the silence; he had a need to know what to expect. "When we get there, what exactly will happen?"

"Well, we'll do whatever has to be done. Maybe help build the fire, set up the lodge, get food together, whatever. After a while, when Blue Star feels it's right, we'll change our clothes and get ready to start the sweat."

The rabbi was startled by this answer. Punctuality was very important to him. He had always made it a point to start services on time. He didn't like to be late and watched his time carefully knowing that he always had many meetings and people to visit. His desire to be on time perhaps was a result of his father usually being late to events. Even at his bar mitzvah his parents arrived late. He was so embarrassed that he vowed to always be on time. It was these thoughts that finally sunk in, prompting him to repeat in a shocked voice, "Do you really mean that we don't know when the sweat will actually begin or when it will end?"

31

Sue's reply was simple. "Exactly. You have some new concepts to learn and one of them is 'Indian Time' which is not based on that thing on your wrist, but more on when things feel right."

The rabbi resorted to his lawyer's training. "Sue, could a doctor run a practice without watching the clock and having specific appointments? How could a lawyer bill for his time or when would I start and end my classes when I was teaching? I understand the desire to be attuned to nature, but this sounds crazy!"

Sue didn't respond and kept driving.

The rabbi was quiet for a moment and then reflected softly, "On the other hand, our mystical tradition does teach that time is not real. It is simply a construct for us humans. G-d sees all time at the same time. Time is not linear but circular and concurrent. What you explained actually does make sense." The rabbi, now more relaxed, continued, "Our rabbis teach that on Shabbat we are to release ourselves of the tyranny of time and get into G-d's rhythm. Maybe I've been out of rhythm," he acknowledged softly, his thoughts wandering.

Talking to no one in particular, he persisted in his discourse. "If time is not real, then we are allowing a totally unnatural construct to control us. When you pray about something that you care about deeply at that moment, you cannot be bound by linear time. When you only pray at specific times regulated by a clock, then you can be out of step with yourself and with your heart."

He smiled, "Enough philosophy for now. But, I would like to know when this sweat finally begins, whatever time that may be, what will happen?"

"Oh, I presume you mean is there a strict ritual? In a matter of speaking, there is a structure that is very unstructured. The sweat has four parts called 'flaps.' Simply put, super heated stones are brought into the lodge, the flap is closed and after a time the flap is open. This takes place four times. Each of the flaps honors one of the four directions. Yet, what happens during the flap varies immensely with those who are present and the energy of the leader. It is an interconnected, organic creation."

The rabbi asked, "Do we pay for the sweat?"

Sue started laughing. First it was a quiet laugh and then the dam burst and she could not stop. When she finally controlled herself-and it took a while-she blurted out, "No! They offer their rituals as gifts and refuse any direct payment."

"Then, how do they live?" the rabbi inquired.

"Sometimes they get jobs monitoring state construction sites that may be near Indian burial grounds. Blue Star is a good jewelry maker and gets some money that way. People give them things-food, clothing, cars. Their way of life is not easy, but they don't sell their spirituality."

Then Sue looked over at the rabbi, cocked her head like an owl and asked him, "Well, Rabbi, do you sometimes feel that you 'sell' spirituality?"

The rabbi was about to say to her that he didn't know what she meant. However, he knew exactly what she meant and liked the openness of their conversation. "Yes, I do charge for doing weddings and funerals. And, the temple does charge for the high holidays - we do charge people to pray. It has always bothered me. I know that I need the money for my family and a temple needs to collect funds so that it can function the rest of the year...it still bothers me though," he concluded softly.

"Give me a break," uttered Ann, lifting her almost empty wine glass. "Temples need money. We could pass the hat I guess. Would you really consider not charging congregants for the high holidays?"

The rabbi considered ignoring this last question. He knew it was going to cause a fight. He could just continue with his story and maybe Ann would let him off the hook that way. No, she wouldn't let him go that easily. So, he jumped in. "Actually, I have been considering not charging for the high holidays and simply asking for donations. I truly think we'll get enough. And if not, we can go out and raise the difference."

"Wait one minute. I thought you were the one who 'hated' to do fundraising. I've heard from many people that you have virtually refused to raise money."

"Yes, I don't like rabbis raising money when it takes away their energy from doing what they are really supposed to do-be religious leaders. In this case, I think that the money issue has gotten too far out of hand and such a policy could actually have a very positive impact on the spirituality of the community. For this I'd help to get the money," the rabbi righteously declared.

"I don't think we'll ever know. The Board would never be willing to take the risk. If they did, I think it would be an interesting experiment that I'd like us to try. In the meantime, on with the story."

They continued the drive in silence. Most people are uncomfortable with silence, needing to rush in with some comment, even if it is stupid. That day, Rabbi Daniels felt comfortable with silence. They respected each other's need to explore their own thoughts in the stillness.

The rabbi was becoming mesmerized by the paved road that looked like an endless ribbon and the monotonous and even hypnotizing effect of the power poles on his right side. Sue finally awakened the rabbi from his trance by pointing to a small lonely building down the road. "There is Gus' Bar and Grill, which means we are getting close. This is where you call to leave messages for the 'preservation.' I always stop to check if they have any messages we should take to Blue Star."

Gus' Bar and Grill was a small-inhabited island in the middle of a dirt ocean. A faded blue wood frame single story rectangular building offered to be an oasis with its handwritten sign announcing "air conditioning" surrounded like bees around a flower advertising "Bud," "Miller," and "Coors." However, this promise seemed flawed when they walked through the torn screen door and were hit by a cloud of smoke. Although it was early afternoon, the air inside had a heavy blue tinge and there appeared to be two or three men already frozen to their seats with the obligatory glass of beer in their hand.

It only took a minute to find out from the bartender that there were no messages to be taken to Blue Star. It took that same amount of time for the rabbi to realize they were on the edge of civilization and where they were going had no phone. He wondered what else it didn't have.

They had been back on the black ribbon of road amongst all the browns for only a matter of seconds when Sue said loudly and without warning, "Hold on! I suggest you start praying now."

The rabbi didn't have time to even understand her words before she turned sharply to the right and they were bumping along a dirt road without any obvious signs. "We'll be on this road for some time," she shouted over the noise of the tires on the gravel.

He really did not trust her car with its rattling muffler and its archeological artifacts. The rabbi was used to driving slowly on dirt roads to protect his car from getting damaged. Sue didn't seem to reduce her speed at all when they left the highway and the cloud of dust that surrounded them made it very hard to see exactly where they were going.

This made Rabbi Daniels think of an old Israeli joke about a rabbi and a bus driver who were both in heaven. The rabbi asked the angel at the entrance to heaven why the bus driver was being allowed in. The angel replied, "You, Rabbi, made people sleep when you worked by giving sermons; however, when the bus driver worked, he made people sincerely pray."

As the car continued to jerk and bump, the rabbi's stomach began to feel nervous. This was like a bad field trip in grammar school, like going to a museum to see a new exhibit that he didn't want to see. Now the rabbi began to feel disquieted and he began to pray. He quickly realized that he was not asking for a safe trip, but his personal prayer had become more intense. He prayed that he would be open to this experience, that he would not be just a museum goer, observing, but that he would be willing to risk being touched by whatever this experience would offer him.

He began to feel better and opened his eyes. He looked out the window and saw a jack rabbit off to the side as well as a tan and brown ground squirrel run into its hole. He saw a cactus plant with its fortress of thorns. He even saw a snake, he thought, moving near the road. He started to smile and the excitement of the journey returned.

And then the car stopped in the middle of the road. At first he wondered if his fears of the car breaking down were coming true. There were no phone lines, no power lines, and no living souls around. Sue got out of the car and the rabbi blindly followed her. He made out a small road to the side with a chain across the dirt path protecting its entrance. Hanging from the chain was a weathered sign, which read:

Owl Preservation of the Antchu Nation
Preserving the Native American Tradition
no drinking - no drugs

Sue easily untied the chain, gave an end to the rabbi and motioned for him to walk back across the road and let the chain fall on the ground. Rabbi Daniels walked to the side of the road letting the chain fall while Sue returned to the car and then drove over the chain onto the side road. The rabbi loosely retied the chain across the road and got back into the car. About three minutes later, he saw four or five mobile trailers of various faded colors that looked like tired old dinosaurs frozen in time on flat rubber tires. There was a large single room structure, which Sue told him was the main hall consisting of a seemingly flimsy construction of a mixture of screens, old doors and recycled plywood.

When the rabbi asked about a small shed with a swinging door, he was told it was the community's main toilet. The small brown shed had been placed atop a large hole dug deep into the ground. There were no electric lines, no phone lines, no water pipes, and no trash. There was nothing to interfere with the view of the deep royal blue sky and there was no sound from incessant televisions or from interfering phones ringing.

"Welcome to the Owl Preservation," Sue declared simply. "Rather different from your synagogue and your home."

"I've heard of 'reservations' but what is a 'preservation?'" the rabbi asked, intrigued.

"A preservation is a private piece of land not given to the Indians by the government. This is five acres that Blue Star and a few others bought to get their families off of the reservation, which had too much liquor and abuse. They wanted to 'preserve' the beauty of the tradition by essentially escaping from the reservation."

She had driven up the road and parked the car while talking. She opened her door and continued, "Why don't you walk around and we'll catch up in a few minutes." Pointing to a fire pit in the distance she stated, "Why don't you go see how the fire is doing?"

"How should a bonfire be doing on a hot summer day?" the rabbi sarcastically asked, but Sue had already left. He walked over and the bronze looking man, in his forties, clad only in some shorts, introduced himself. "I'm Morning Breeze, the fire keeper."

"I'm Rabbi Daniels, a friend of Sue's," the rabbi replied, thinking how stuffy and unwelcoming he was acting. "Can you tell me a little of what you are doing?" He felt like a reporter but there was no camera following him. He was clearly out of his element.

Morning Breeze didn't seem to mind. He was placing more wood into the pit and spoke softly over the sound of the wood cackling. "First there was the fire. We place stones on the base of the fire and then continue to add wood so the fire is strong and makes the stones very, very hot. We call these stones grandfathers as they are the voice of our ancestors." He then made a prayer and spread sage and sweet grass over the fire. Rabbi Daniels watched intently until the small fire grew quite large into a roaring blaze of reds and blues and yellows.

The sweat lodge itself was just beyond the fire pit and resembled a large, upside down woven basket. Several woolen blankets of varying colors with holes and frayed ends had been placed over the large bowl shaped frame made of willow saplings. The layering was to insure that no sunlight would pierce the structure's outer layer and that the heat would linger inside. The rabbi saw another, yet much older Indian get on his hands and knees and enter the sweat lodge. He closed the flap for a while and came out calling to

Morning Breeze as he walked away, "You built a strong sweat and I didn't see any sunlight when I closed the flaps. We will have a good sweat today."

Morning Breeze came up behind the rabbi and whispered into his ear, "That is Blue Star and he will be leading the sweat." The rabbi noticed a rather short, dark skinned man whose age was hard to tell but who obviously had a powerful build. "He is a great man and you will enjoy his teachings. He went inside and closed the flap to inspect the sweat lodge and make sure that it was absolutely dark inside so that the darkness will let our souls come out." The rabbi nodded and thought that darkness can be a good vehicle to interrupt the natural focus on the physical and help one's attention move more to the spiritual.

During the drive he had asked Sue about how the sweat lodge was made. She told him that Blue Star and Morning Breeze would gather twelve young willow saplings. Each sapling was cut with great care only after asking its permission to be used. Tobacco would then be spread on the poles to show thanks for their sacrifice. The saplings were bent and tied together at the top to form a square representing the four directions. Additional poles were added to both give the structure strength and to represent the arch of father sky. She continued, "Willows were traditionally used for sweat lodges due to their strength. Moreover, they grow close to the water, which has the power to cleanse, purify and enliven the spirit."

The rabbi had listened to this explanation and added, "Water represents spiritual as well as physical nourishment in the Jewish tradition. It is a metaphor for such things as wisdom, tradition, rebirth, connection, and growth. The Jews had to pass through water, the Red Sea, to be reborn into freedom. Water is often associated with women and all of the matriarchs somehow are portrayed as ones who bring or protect the water. Water gives life, as do our mothers. When the Biblical Sarah dies, there is no water, no spirit. The people are lost until another matriarch can help guide them spiritually and then they find water again."

The rabbi then noticed that the entire area around the sweat lodge was very clean. It was as if someone had carefully raked the area. Sue had earlier explained that this area is considered sacred and that the leader of the sweat is very careful to make sure that it is not contaminated. When the area was

37

initially cleared and Blue Star knew that he was going to build a sweat lodge, he and Morning Breeze would have taken smoldering white sage and danced around the area to create and enclose a sacred space. Blue Star is so protective of this area that he makes sure there is always someone nearby. If he ever leaves, a member of his family is present or someone else is always nearby the land. She had emphasized that the land is never left alone.

Rabbi Daniels was startled from his contemplation by loud voices that seemed angry. He turned his head in an attempt to locate the direction of the noise and saw two men, recognizing one as Blue Star. The other man was much taller and also had long hair. He was jabbing at Blue Star with his hands. There were strange lights coming from his hands, and then the rabbi realized the lights were merely reflections from rings on his fingers. Soon the man left and got into a new looking BMW and drove off, leaving a trail of dust that engulfed Blue Star.

The rabbi noted that Sue was approaching him and had changed into a simple pair of denim shorts, a blue T-shirt and a pair of sandals.

"So, you've met Morning Breeze and Blue Star," she said.

The rabbi was still staring at Blue Star who began to move off. "Well, I've talked a little to Morning Breeze. He told me that Blue Star was very special and would be running the 'sweat,'" the rabbi replied somewhat absentmindedly. "Do you know who that man was that was just talking to Blue Star?"

"Sorry, I didn't see anyone," replied Sue. "What did you think of Morning Breeze?"

The rabbi was bothered by the interaction he just witnessed and really didn't know why. Sue continued, "Morning Breeze is also very special. He's on the tribal council and is considered by many as an elder, almost as knowledgeable as Grandfather White Eagle, even though he is still youthful. His role as fire keeper is a great honor and must be done very carefully for the sweat to work well."

"So, who was that guy?"

"I don't know. I had forgotten about him until I was telling you the story just now. Probably not important," the rabbi replied.

"What about the chief? Do we finally get to meet White Eagle? What was he like when you met him?"

"Sorry, Ann, I didn't meet White Eagle for quite awhile after that. However, what I realized at the sweat was just how important he was to this community. He didn't have to be present to have a powerful impact," the rabbi observed. "I wonder what people say about me when I'm not around?"

Ann coughed a little, "You really want to know?"

"Now that you put it that way, I guess not. Do you think people will really miss me when I'm gone?"

"Some will and some won't. Don't play the numbers game. You can't and you haven't pleased everyone. But you've pleased a lot. There are a lot of good people who will miss you. If your ego has now been satisfied, will you please continue?" pleaded Ann.

"Did you bring that pouch of tobacco I asked you to bring?" Sue asked.

"Yes, and why do I feel so ridiculous giving this to the leader of the sweat?" When Sue had him bring tobacco as a gift to the sweat, he thought it was very strange. He had been taught about the evils of tobacco, including that it causes cancer. Whenever he saw a baseball player chewing a mouthful of tobacco and then spitting it out, he would think, "How disgusting." But Sue had told him that for the Native Americans, tobacco is a healing substance of great power. For example, when Blue Star's son got a cut on his finger, she saw him put some tobacco in his mouth, then put the moistened tobacco on the cut of his son's finger and hold it there by tying a white piece of cloth around the wound. Sue told him the finger healed quite quickly and nicely.

Sue looked behind the rabbi and remarked, "Blue Star is coming and this would be a good time to give him the tobacco. This is serious. Just present it to him."

Rabbi Daniels reached into his pocket. Friday afternoon he had gone to a small grocery store owned by a couple that emigrated from Iraq and asked for a pouch of their best pipe tobacco. He was given a cellophane covered paper pouch with the name Captain Jack for $2.45. The rabbi felt in his pocket and took out the plastic pouch. He felt awkward knowing that he was giving this spiritual man something with so little apparent value. Nevertheless, he held out the cellophane package to the approaching short, weathered man, who wore faded blue jeans, a well-worn denim shirt, and a red bandana over his long white hair. Blue Star stopped in front of the rabbi, did not say a word, took the tobacco with great honor and looked for a long time into the rabbi's eyes. All the rabbi could do was continue to stare into those deep brown pools with a profound and lingering gaze. The rabbi thought of the pain and anguish of these people being forced out of their lands, their traditions disregarded, and yet all he saw in those eyes was kindness and gentleness. There was no judgment in those eyes, just curiosity. Blue Star, after a while, broke the eye contact and carefully placed the package on a dirt mound next to a skeleton of a cow's head, some eagle feathers, antlers, beads, and a pair of glasses, forming an altar next to the fire pit and the sweat lodge.

Blue Star then embraced and startled the rabbi by saying, "You are now my brother." It felt awkward to Rabbi Daniels and yet it felt right. He liked Blue Star immediately and felt that they were kindred spirits.

The rabbi, now noticing the altar more carefully after the tobacco had been placed on it, asked Blue Star, "I somewhat understand many of the objects on the altar. But, a pair of black plastic framed glasses? This I don't understand."

An affectionate smile crossed Blue Star's face, like a rainbow after a spring shower. "White Eagle, our community's elder, has taught that we need to use not only traditional items on our altar, but to place modern objects as well. He wants us to find the connection between the old and the new. These glasses belong to Morning Breeze who placed them on the altar this morning to help him see the truth. The objects on this altar will help guide the sweat today."

Rabbi Daniels smiled. Blue Star also was attempting to combine his ancient tradition with modern concepts. Rabbi Daniels also needed guidance. He asked, "Would it be okay if I added my *kippah* to the altar? The *kippah* represents for me the presence of G-d as a force of wisdom and direction." Blue Star nodded and the rabbi took off his head covering, placing the black circle of cloth with its blue band next to the glasses.

Blue Star then asked with a smile emanating from his eyes, "I've always wanted to ask a rabbi how it stays on your head."

The rabbi, now in a more relaxed mood, answered, "That's a trade secret. Many people use a bobby pin, others a hair clip. I, on the other hand..." the rabbi paused dramatically, lifted up his *kippah* from the altar and handed it to Blue Star.

Blue Star turned the head covering over and concluded in surprise, "It's Velcro."

"It sticks nicely to my hair, except in strong wind," the rabbi added as Blue Star carefully returned the *kippah* to the altar.

While they had been talking, the rabbi had been aware of the sound of cars pulling up and now saw several people approaching the sweat area. Sue had reappeared at his elbow. "The sweat will start soon; it's time for you to change." The rabbi was directed to the changing area that consisted of some old, weather-beaten doors nailed together to give limited protection from inquisitive eyes. He emerged wearing red swim trucks and a blue tee with the inscription of "Temple Shalom Pre-School." Other participants had already changed and were quietly mingling in front of the sweat lodge. The rabbi counted eighteen people; a holy number in the Jewish tradition that represents Chai, life. This indeed was going to be a very special experience.

41

The rabbi had marveled that Ann had been so quiet for so long. He wasn't surprised when she now asked, "I've always wondered why 18 means life? I don't get it."

"First, I want to acknowledge that you've been able to keep quiet for more than a second. Well done. I think you're making progress."

"Don't try to get on my good side, it won't work. Now answer the question," Ann replied.

"Ignoring your lack of respect for the rabbi, I don't understand how you know so much about so many things but know so little about Judaism. You've worked at the temple for a long time. I don't get it."

"Look, my parents were Jewish by name only and never, I mean never, took religion very seriously. They didn't send me to Sunday school, we never observed the holidays and I never had a bat mitzvah. I fear that I only knew that Jews ate lox and bagels. That's gastronomic Judaism. I am one very ignorant Jew. One reason I chose to come to work at the temple was the hope that I would learn about my tradition. I thought working in a Jewish environment around rabbis and educators would teach me a lot about who I am. Frankly, I haven't learned very much over the years. The previous two rabbis were not exactly spiritual people; they didn't have time to be bothered answering my questions, and I really didn't want to learn from them. I never had time to attend any of the classes and I felt it would be awkward being in classes with congregants. They would quickly see that I didn't know very much and I'd be embarrassed. So, I have a lot of stored up questions and I want some answers. So, start teaching!" Ann concluded in a demanding tone.

"Well, if you put it that way, I have no choice but to teach you," Rabbi Daniels was now smiling. "And Ann, I am honored that you want to learn from me. A numerical value is associated with each of the twenty-two Hebrew letters. This is called *gematria*. The first Hebrew letter is *aleph* and also stands for the number one. *Bet*, the second letter is naturally tied to the number two, and so on. Accordingly, if we take the word for life *chai*, it is made up of two Hebrew letters, the *yod* and the *chect*. *Yod* as the value ten with *chect* valued at eight. Put them together, you have 18."

"I understood that," admitted Ann. "But, why will the temple sometimes get donations of 36 dollars or even 360 dollars?"

Chai is such a powerful concept that often people give gifts in increments of 18. Hence the 36, 72, etc. I love playing with numbers and words. There really is a connection that opens up the possibility for greater understanding."

"Okay, you may go on now," directed Ann.

The rabbi saw that a somewhat relaxed line was forming in front of the sweat lodge. He was happy this was going to be a mixed sweat. Sue had told him they have sweats for men, women, and mixed. If the rabbi had come for an all male one, he would have had to go in naked. The rabbi was somewhat of a prude and the Jewish tradition had notions of modesty, so he felt more comfortable wearing clothing in this alien place with its own customs. He also knew that he was generally the type to go into things carefully, inching himself into a swimming pool, unlike those who jumped in fearlessly. Nevertheless, it was fascinating to him that he was willingly "jumping" into this new situation.

Morning Breeze stood before the open flap with a bundle of smoldering sage. As the rabbi approached, he got his first whiff of this pungent smell, which was very foreign but soothing at the same time. He noticed the women were lined up first and as each one approached the flap, Morning Breeze would pass the sage around their bodies and then under each foot as it was raised. Finally, the rabbi's turn came and Morning Breeze passed the sage around the rabbi's body; then he was asked to first lift his right foot for the sage to pass under and then his left foot. Ritual and order were important and the rabbi wanted to be respectful. He felt that he was entering into a sacred process and was silent.

He got down on his knees and crawled into the dark belly of the sweat lodge. It felt to him as if he was entering into the womb of mother earth, warm and embracing. At the same time, he also thought of Jonah going into the belly of the whale; it was foreign and perilous, and he had no idea if he would be bored out of his mind or scared out of his wits. Although it took a few moments for his eyes to adjust, he saw that all the women were already seated around the rim of the lodge to his right and he was being motioned to move clockwise towards his left and sit next to a rather large man. He tensed up, a little afraid. He didn't particularly like crowded, hot, and dark places, all of which he was now experiencing.

He sat down cross legged on hard ground and knew that he was soon going to be very sore. He already felt hot in the tightly packed lodge and wondered just how much hotter it was going to get.

With no talking, Blue Star, bare-chested and with his long hair released from its containment by the red bandana now hanging lazily on his shoulders, came in first and sat near the entrance to the tent. He now mo-

43

tioned to Morning Breeze. A hot stone was brought to the door of the sweat lodge in an old rusty shovel. Blue Star then picked up the stone with antlers and carefully placed it in an indentation in the center of the sweat lodge. The antlers felt more appropriate than the shovel to the rabbi. On the other hand, who was he to decide what was and was not a ritual object? He smiled with greater appreciation as well as with increasing apprehension as the process was followed six more times until seven stones lay side by side in the center of the lodge. The rabbi took mental note of the numbers. Seven is a very spiritual number in many traditions, and it often represents creation, renewal, and balance. Seven appears throughout the Jewish tradition. G-d created the world in six days and then rested on the seventh. Seven days in a week and seven lower spheres in the Jewish mystical system. There are many Biblical injunctions about the land that came to mind such as the sabbatical year where the land gets to rest every seven years. He saw the seven rocks and immediately made the connection. Seven was a perfect number to begin a sweat. He wondered if numbers played the same role in the Native American tradition.

After the seven stones were gathered in the center of the lodge, a pail of water was brought in by Morning Breeze and jointly lifted by Blue Star and Morning Breeze to touch the stones and then it was placed next to Blue Star. He spread some of the bluish gray sage and greenish sweet grass over the stones and the smell rose again. This time the smell was not foreign and the rabbi began to relax. His growing sense of comfort, however, was jolted as the flap was closed and the lodge was plunged into total darkness except for a red glow coming from the hot rocks in the center.

He really did feel like he was in the belly of a whale and didn't know how he would emerge from this experience. Would he be able to tolerate the heat which he had been warned would be so intense? What about the spiritual journey? Would he be comfortable with the tradition or would he remain the outsider looking in through the bars of his own perceptions? Another feeling arose that he did not expect. He was alone even though he was surrounded by many souls. He knew that whatever happened would be a very personal voyage, as he sensed there was great power in what was about to happen.

"There are four directions which we will be honoring with our four flaps." Blue Star began to speak from across the room. He could not be seen, but the rabbi felt his voice as a calming presence. The importance of honoring and seeing spiritual significance was familiar to the rabbi. During one of the three Jewish pilgrimage festivals called Sukkot, one shakes a combination of palm branches, willows, myrtle, and *etrog*, a citrus that looks somewhat like a lemon, in the four directions as well as up and down. One also builds a temporary structure covered by palm branches or other green leafy branches. Unlike the opaque sweat lodge, one has to be able to see stars at night.

Blue Star now began a chant with a drumbeat. The rabbi had presumed he was well acquainted with Indian drumbeats from all the westerns he had watched as a child. He was wrong. The beat was different, more sophisticated, richer and clearly profoundly spiritual. There was a rhythm that spoke to him of the ancestors, both from the Native American tradition and from his own. It was as if the singing was coming from the earth through Blue Star. And, although Blue Star had put some water on the stones to create heat, it was not too intense. "This isn't too bad," thought the rabbi as a smug smile came across his face. "I can do this," he assured himself.

After what seemed like a short time to the rabbi, Blue Star opened the flap and a cool breeze came in. The sunlight streaming in allowed people to look at one another and exchange smiles. Sue, who was sitting in the woman's section, smiled at the rabbi and he smiled back.

There was no standing, but the rabbi let his legs untangle to give them a quick stretch. Then Blue Star closed the flap and spoke: "The second flap is dedicated to the South, the sun and the color yellow." He then startled Rabbi Daniels, saying, "Grandfather White Eagle has always taught that we are to honor spiritual teachers. Each people have elders who hold their community's wisdom. We have another spiritual leader, an elder of the Jewish people with us, a rabbi. Would you please honor us with a song from your tradition about nature?" Rabbi Daniels panicked. It wasn't very hot in the lodge, yet he started to perspire. He realized that he didn't know any song about nature, not really. In a very real sense, he had come to the sweat to find a stronger link to nature and here Blue Star presumed that he already had a strong connection. He was here to learn, not to teach.

And then words started to emerge from his mouth, almost involuntarily. These words, written by a young girl who had been killed during World War II, were about the unity of hope, the wonder of nature and prayer. The words came out hesitantly and softly and then gathered strength. This young girl had lived in what would later be called Israel and had parachuted behind German lines to try to save stranded Jewish children. She was caught, tortured and killed. Her voice was now living through the rabbi in this most unusual and yet appropriate setting. He sang in Hebrew:

Ei-li, Ei-li, she-lo yi-ga-meir le-ol-am...

And then in English
"Oh Lord, My G-d, I pray that these things never end:
The sand and the sea,
The rush of the waters,
The crash of the heavens
The prayer of the heart."

During the song, Blue Star began to drum softly. When he finished there was only stillness. At first Rabbi Daniels felt uncomfortable, and then the silence felt embracing. It held and cradled him like a loving mother. He had already learned from Blue Star about the equality and connection between nature and humans. Blue Star spoke of the equality of spirit between plants, animals, rocks and wind, as well as between the two-legged, four-legged, and the winged creatures. This was so different from the typical hierarchical view and sense of superiority and dominance found in the "Western" traditions of humans to animals, of humans to nature. He had just had a glimpse of this in his tradition while he was singing. The rabbi was so caught up that he didn't even notice the second flap had ended until light again emerged from the open entrance.

He now became aware that a bottle of water was being passed around and many were drinking. He also saw that it was being passed clockwise to follow the season, the same way they had first entered the lodge. He was feeling so good and confident that he passed it along without drinking. The heat wasn't bothering him; he could take it and didn't need water. The rabbi became a little startled when he looked around and became aware that some people seemed to be suffering under the heat and were drinking greedily from the water bottle. Then he noticed the man next to him had taken off his shirt and had ugly scars above his nipples.

The rabbi realized this man was a sun dancer, although he did not look Native American. He didn't know much about this tradition except what he had read. He knew the sun dancing tradition included tying hooks to one's flesh, which were torn away while dancing. His first reaction was one of repulsion. In the Jewish tradition, one does not desecrate the body with flagellation or scarring. Yet, he admitted to himself that he was intrigued. This person had to have been in a deep spiritual state to have suffered the obvious pain and was willing to be scarred for life with this statement of devotion. He strangely felt honored and somewhat humbled to be sitting next to a sun dancer.

47

As the third flap was about to begin, the rabbi felt an unexpected sense of apprehension. When the flap was closed for the third session, the rabbi could not shake a feeling of panic. He actually wanted to run out, to escape. He didn't understand. He had survived the first two sessions easily and had felt cocky. As the now familiar sizzling sound of water hitting rocks began, the heat seemed to rush at him like a wave overpowering his senses. The heat felt unbearably oppressive and his breathing increased. Yet every breath meant hot, searing steam entering his lungs. He was choking from the heat and his nostrils were burning with each breath. It was too much. He knew that Blue Star was talking about the third direction and its color. But he could only hear the sound of his beating heart and feel the heat. His mind started screaming, "What am I doing here, who am I kidding! Get out, just jump up and run!"

Out of desperation more than anything else, he started to use a spiritual mediation that he had rather recently learned based on the *Sh'ma*, "Listen Israel, the Lord your G-d is one." These six Hebrew words from the Bible are considered the central prayer in the Jewish tradition and may originally have been a mantra. He took a shallow breath and mentally whispered the first two words of the prayer. Then he slowly breathed out while focusing on the next two words and then breathed in again thinking of the last two words.

He continued this meditation to the point where his total concentration was on his breath. He was able to feel that he was breathing in G-d's breath and that his breathing and presence at that lodge at that time was part of the divine plan. The rabbi became so relaxed that he was soon able to concentrate on Blue Star's words about this flap representing the West and our unceasing movement toward maturity and understanding. He even began smiling as he realized his panic had reminded him to be humble in the presence of this ancient and powerful ritual. This time, when this flap ended, he joined the others in drinking fully from the water bottle being passed around.

While the flap was open, a young girl, probably in her early twenties with blond hair and a tie-dyed shirt, started to look very pale, got up, and not too easily, left. An older man, sitting near the entrance, smiled at us all, stood with the aid of Blue Star and left. The rabbi wondered if maybe he should be joining them as his previous good mood took flight and his confidence waned. He was hungry to surrender to the full experience and the heat; the fire was not alien fire. Images from the Bible about the transformational power of fire kept running through his mind; Moses and the burning bush, the Jews being guided in the desert by a flame during the night and the light in each synagogue to represent G-d's eternal presence. He was going to remain. He wondered if the sweat lodge would provide the alchemical crucible his soul had been seeking.

Just as stones were brought in to begin each of the previous flaps, five additional stones, called "grandfathers" by Blue Star, were brought in on the rusty shovel. The rabbi wondered why White Eagle was often referred to as a "grandfather," just like the stones. He presumed that the title represented those who embody some ancient wisdom. Morning Breeze carefully picked up each one of the scorching rocks and expertly placed them on top of the stones that had already been piled up in the middle. Fresh water had been put into the dented and rusty aluminum bucket. Blue Star and Morning Breeze picked up the bucket together and carefully touched its bottom to the searing stone that had just been placed on the top of the pile as a sort of blessing. The bucket was then taken by Blue Star and placed next to him. Sweet grass and pungent sage were placed on the new stones. The rabbi deeply breathed in the aroma and felt intoxicated by the smells. Using his hands in a scooping motion, as he had seen so many do, he tried to bring more of the smell into his spirit. The flap was closed and they were again plunged into total darkness.

Blue Star explained, "This last flap is to honor the North and the teachers who guided our footsteps but are no longer physically with us." As he poured water on the stones and the heat began to rise, the rabbi started his breathing meditation using the *Sh'ma* again. After a song of honor, Blue Star asked, "Please share names, and invite the souls in, of people you wish to honor." He was quiet as he poured more water on the stone and the heat increased. The first man to the far right of Rabbi Daniels started, "I bring in my grandmother who recently died. She was my teacher and always loved me no matter what I did." A woman across from the rabbi spoke next. "I bring in my mother. She loved me very much, no matter what I did. I miss her so much," and she started to softly cry. The rabbi then spoke into the darkness, "I invite... my wife who died two years ago. She taught me to try... to try different things and not be afraid." The rabbi had been thinking about his Leah and wondered once again why she had to die and leave him alone. She loved to read and discuss theology, and her favorite book from the Bible was the book of Job. She had told him that it was the one Biblical story she had never fully understood. After Leah's death, he wasn't sure he understood it either. The rabbi had once co-taught with a nun the book of Job in the theology department. It was a wonderful experience as he taught and learned about questions that often don't have answers and journeys that are important even though the destination may not be reached. Perhaps it was the journey that was in truth the real destination.

The rabbi was becoming more aware of the heat and mentally began to beg the speakers to keep their remarks short, as the heat was beating him. Finally, Blue Star opened the flap; the rabbi crawled, clockwise, out of the sweat. He had survived. And, he felt refreshed.

When everyone was out of the sweat, Sue came over to the rabbi with a smile. "Well?" she said.

"It was great...no, it was special. Is it always this spiritual?"

Sue thought for a moment. "No. There are times when I feel really connected and other times when I don't. However, each one is different and unique in its own way. This was your first one and you will always have this memory."

"I've never been called an "elder" before. I've been called a rabbi, a religious leader, and other things. But, this is the first time. Truthfully, it felt good." Rabbi Daniels then startled Sue with a Hebrew prayer called *Shehecheyanu*. "*Baruch ata...*" When he finished he declared, "We do a special blessing when something new happens. You are right, new things are special and they help us to renew our appreciation of life and its wonder. Loosely translated, the prayer means, Blessed are you, Ruler of the universe, who gave us life, nurtured us and brought us to this special time and place.

"Are you hungry?" Sue asked.

Surprisingly, the rabbi hadn't noticed that he was very hungry, even ravenous. They changed back into their regular clothing and entered the large meeting room, which had a variety of food on a center table surrounded by an assortment of chairs. Everyone had brought food and the combination of the bags of potato chips, pots of beans, plates of doughnuts, blocks of yellow and white cheeses, various salads, and pots of soup created a large bounty of colors and smells. The rabbi, while not a great cook, had made a chili *relleno* pie that soon became a mere memory as it was the first dish to be emptied. Prior to anyone eating, the rabbi noticed a rather young woman with pale white skin taking a plate and putting a small portion from all the foods at the potluck on it and then leaving.

Sue saw the rabbi following the woman with his eyes. "That is Carol, Blue Star's wife. The plate will be left outside somewhere as an offering."

The rabbi was lost in thought. She didn't appear to be a Native American and she was significantly younger than Blue Star. Within the Jewish tradition, there was a strong emphasis to marry within the tradition for a variety of reasons, including the obvious one that there were so few Jews. Rabbi Daniels had presumed the same for Native Americans. Maybe he was wrong.

As if Sue was reading his mind, she inquired, "You're probably wondering about Carol. I don't fully understand why, but many of the tribe elders marry younger women who are often not Indians. I'm sure there is a lot of psychology in this, but I don't get it. On the other hand, though, you will love Carol-she is so full of energy."

As if out of nowhere, a woman's voice interrupted their conversation, "Sorry, but I couldn't help overhearing what you were saying. It is strange."

"I'm sorry, have we met?" Sue replied in a formal manner that was not typical for her.

A rather short woman who was dressed in an all white dress with her long hair pulled back by a black leather thong replied, "I was with you in the sweat. I personally don't have anything against all of you coming to our ceremonies, but we have so few men. You should leave them alone." With that she turned and walked away.

Sue was so shocked that she just stared after the woman. The rabbi was also looking and interjected, "There was a lot of resentment behind that statement. I've heard these types of feelings expressed before. When you're a minority, like us Jews, there is a fear of people marrying outside the religion or in this case, outside the tribe." Before the rabbi could continue, Blue Star approached.

"Thank you for coming. You're the first rabbi we've had here. You did well in the heat and I hope that someday you will meet our elder, White Eagle."

When the rabbi tried to thank Blue Star and say he was happy he had decided to come, he was stopped short. "You really had no choice. The Great Spirit wanted you to be here. There is a reason you are here."

Chapter 4

White Eagle

Who is wise? One who learns from all people.
Mishnah

A nn got up and stretched with her arms pointing to the sky. She covered a yawn with her hand. "A good story, very interesting, but when do we meet White Eagle? And, where is dessert?"

Rabbi Daniels looked at his watch and noticed that it was closing in on 9pm. He was feeling quite good and relaxed after the wine and the full meal. He rarely drank, and certainly never this much. He took a towel off the counter in the kitchen and draped it over his arm and with a rather poor French accent said, "Would the madam like tea with her dessert?" He then proceeded to pick up the dishes and pile them in the sink. He filled the tea-kettle with water, turned on the stove, and began rummaging through the refrigerator to see if there was any dessert. He presumed that amongst all the food left, there had to be something sweet. He was not disappointed. After a few minutes, he presented Ann with a steaming cup of Earl Grey tea along with a large slice of cheesecake as well as a similar portion for himself. He sat down once again on the stool in the kitchen, which by now had become uncomfortable. "How about we move to a more comfortable location?"

With that he picked up his teacup and cake plate and led the way to the social hall. The room was dark except for a few lights the rabbi had turned on as they entered the vast room, which was filled with empty tables and chairs. The remnants of the wedding were still somewhat visible in the form of errant white balloons trapped under the high ceiling. They sat down at one of the tables and the rabbi took a sip from his warm tea.

Ann was eying the rabbi as she took a drink. "If you are looking, searching for something, why Native American? There are a lot of other religious traditions-Buddhism, Islam, Christianity..."

"To be honest, I want to study all these traditions. They all have much to teach."

"Are you trying to find the 'truth'?" she asked.

"No."

"What? If not the truth, then what?" Ann asked, somewhat miffed.

"I believe there is no 'one' truth. Each of our religious traditions has certain pieces. And, even if we were to put the pieces all together, we would still not have a complete picture. G-d is greater than the totality of any one philosophy or religion. And knowing this, I love Judaism. It is truly an incredible, magnificent tradition. Nevertheless, that does not stop me from wanting to learn from these other traditions. It's actually exciting. I've gone to various religious services, retreats and done a lot of interfaith programs. So, I went to the sweat simply because the occasion arose. Since I don't believe in coincidences, I presumed there was a reason for me to go with Sue. So, I went."

Ann, still looking at the rabbi, considered what he had just revealed. "So, what do you think the reason was for you to go to the sweat?"

"I'm not sure the cosmos are that easy to decipher. And many times one doesn't know until hindsight, if ever. Take Joseph, for instance, who was thrown into a pit by his brothers, then sold into slavery, then slammed into prison and then elevated to a royal advisor to the Pharaoh. He eventually saw all those events were leading him to a position where he could save his family from starvation. Only in hindsight did he see all the pieces tied together, connected for a purpose. Maybe we don't see G-d's hand in our lives until we look in the rearview mirror. In all candor, I must admit that at the time I thought I went to learn about how Native Americans view animals."

"You're scaring me," Ann acknowledged with some amusement in her voice.

"I had been thinking about our own treatment of animals. You know, obviously we eat meat, but eating kosher meat should help us have a more respectful attitude towards animals. For example, we can't eat food that was hunted, since the animal was probably killed with excessive pain. Kosher animals like cows must be domesticated and killed with the least amount of pain. But we do eat meat and so do the Native Americans. At the sweat, I talked with Blue Star about his view of animals. I must admit the idea that birds, coyotes, plants and stones are on the same level as we two-legged creatures does not fit in with the Jewish view of this world or, for that matter, Christian and other vertically hierarchical belief systems. But, it was interesting. It challenged me. Certainly Jacob blessed his sons using images of animals and we children, especially in Israel, are given animal names such as lion or wolf. But our theological system does not countenance the need to listen to animals." Rabbi Daniels paused and looked up at the ceiling. "But to be honest, part of me does resonate with the concept that animals are also spiritual beings that are here to teach us. I can't unequivocally accept the notion of spiritual equality, but neither do I discount it." He paused again and took a sip of his tea.

"So, I first thought I had gone there to get another theological view. Later I thought it was to help them not be evicted from their land."

"Hold on there, Rabbi. I don't know anything yet about White Eagle and now you're talking about them being thrown off their land."

Rabbi Daniels took another swallow of his tea and then a bite of cheese-cake. "Well, I have to get back to Sue for a moment to continue the story. As you are aware, she comes every two weeks for our free-flowing discussions. She attends the weekly Sunday evening course in basic Judaism and then she sees me privately, which all potential converts are required to do. She's not very happy about all the time this is taking. She constantly tells me to say some blessing and make her Jewish. And I continually respond that a conversion to Judaism, like being Jewish, is a journey both of knowledge and passion. And this is a journey that takes time. Some things are better done unhurriedly so they can seep into your mind, your body, and your soul. Anyway, a while ago, at the end of one of our sessions in my office, we played our usual game where she tells me to convert her and I tell her 'not yet.'"

"Sue, the race is not always to the swift. You need to learn the Jewish rhythm of holidays and the Jewish calendar. You need to understand Jewish rituals such as how to celebrate Shabbat and then begin to observe

Shabbat. I want you to taste Jewish foods and begin to cook some of our traditional delicacies from matzo balls to challah. And, I want you to learn how to read and understand basic Hebrew so you can more fully participate in the services."

Sue had heard of all this before, but she was impatient. "All of this I can learn later, and you know that I'll continue to learn."

Rabbi Daniels smiled. "But there is the passion. The 'why's' as I call it. I want you to know deeply why you are choosing to be Jewish. That part of joining us is to better appreciate your own personal spiritual journey. These, and many more personal questions, are better explored privately and carefully."

Sue, somewhat resigned, got up to leave. She stopped and faced the rabbi. "Blue Star told me to invite you to their powwow taking place this weekend up at a lake. He wants you to meet White Eagle. It is just a short drive from here. Your kids would love it too. I can't be there; otherwise I'd offer to drive." The rabbi gave Sue a strange look that made her respond and laugh at the same time, "OK, I won't offer to drive again. Anyway, I'll give you directions. It's on Saturday and Sunday."

The rabbi had been walking over to check out his schedule for the weekend when he stopped and looked at Sue with a cockeyed look, tilting his face to the right. "Oh, sorry," Sue said a little embarrassed. "I know that you won't go on Saturday because of Shabbat. Maybe Sunday?"

Rabbi Daniels chuckled and without looking up replied, "Well, there is Sunday school and an evening wedding. I could get away for a few hours if it's really close by."

With that, Sue wrote out the directions and left the rabbi's office.

It took some negotiations, but finally the kids agreed to go on an outing to the powwow. This was not easy. Since Leah had died -- actually, since before she died, all three of his children had said at one time or another that he was too busy. They wanted more of his time. He could often feel their resentment when the phone rang during dinner and he would have to deal with some emergency. They knew he did important things, but weren't they important as well? Leah had been a good mediator and had been able to give the kids more attention. Since she had died, he did his best, but he knew

55

it wasn't enough. The rabbi sold them on going to the powwow by talking about this as a family outing without any congregants, the interesting food and Indian dancing. Right after religious school, the family piled into their Honda Odyssey and began what he was told would be about a forty-five minute drive up the mountain road behind St. Luke's and through pine covered trees to Lake Gibbon.

The rabbi had never been to a powwow and really didn't know how to answer all the questions being hurled like javelins by his children as they left St. Luke's and began their uphill climb. He was happy they were going. His children, he hoped, would not grow up thinking that all Indians were like those they saw on television, always attacking covered wagons. He also wanted to see Blue Star again and learn more about the Indian tradition.

Before long, he was following a long line of cars up the main road and onto a dirt road. Then he saw Carol, Blue Star's wife, up ahead directing traffic. She was wearing a white cotton dress with a red sash. He didn't think she would remember him as they only briefly spoke at the sweat lodge. She gave him a big grin and waved.

She walked over to his window, saying, "Blue Star told me you might come." She peered into the car and her smile grew as she saw the kids, Zac and Rachael in the back and Adam in front. "Hello and welcome to the Daniels family. You are in for a wonderful treat. You came early."

She must have noticed that he was puzzled by her comment so she continued, "Oh, most people won't be here for another hour or so. We run things here on Indian time, which means all times are approximate, and usually late."

The rabbi nodded and quipped, "All times are relative."

Carol smiled again. "Please park over there." She pointed to her right and continued, "Then follow those people up the hill to the meeting area. Up there is the dance area, a lot of food stands, and an amphitheater for some educational programs. Make sure you hear White Eagle. He is the main elder for the Antchu Nation."

Before she could finish, Zac asked, "Are they selling any bows and arrows?" The rabbi was mortified by this question. All the way up, Zac had been talking about bows and arrows while Rachael, Zac's twin, was asking if she could buy a real Indian dress. The rabbi had done his best to deflect these questions and focus their attention on seeing Native dances and learning more about the Indian culture. Obviously, the rabbi realized his efforts had failed.

However, Carol didn't seem to mind and her smile grew even bigger as she responded, "Sure, there are several stands selling bows and arrows and other Indian items. I have to go back and help direct traffic, but you'll see Blue Star around the dance area and I'll be up there later."

The rabbi noticed his oldest son, Adam, had been quiet. He looked behind and saw him reading 'World Series Highlights.' "Adam," Rabbi Daniels called. No response. "Adam, hello, this is your *Abba*." Again, no response. "In what ball park did Babe Ruth point to a spot in the outfield and then proceed to hit a homer in that direction?" Adam, without looking up, answered, "Wrigley Field in Chicago." "What year?" the Rabbi asked. This time Adam looked up smiling and said, "1932."

As the rabbi and his family walked up the hill after parking the van, he was somewhat surprised to see people of all different ages, races and nationalities. It was like they were all going to a big party, and he guessed they were. On the top of the hill he saw Blue Star wearing the same red bandana to keep his hair back. He came over to the rabbi and called out, "Brother, it is good to see you." With that, he gave the rabbi a big hug.

Rabbi Daniels was again surprised by such a warm reception. It certainly felt uncomfortable to the rabbi the first few times Blue Star used that term back at the sweat. And, the rabbi generally didn't trust people who were too friendly too quickly. However, with Blue Star it felt authentic. It actually felt good and he felt honored to be welcomed in such an affectionate fashion. He returned the hug with enthusiasm.

Blue Star pointed over to the amphitheater and said, "I can see White Eagle is about to begin teaching. You shouldn't miss him. He's a great man. I told him about you."

That last comment surprised the rabbi. He turned around to see a man he guessed to be in his late sixties with stark white hair. There was already a small group of people in the amphitheater and it appeared that the program would be starting soon.

Blue Star continued, "I'll be over with the dancers. Right now we're cleansing the area with white sage. Come over when you finish, but please be careful not to enter the dance area."

When he tried to get Rachael and Zac to come with him to hear White Eagle, all they wanted to do was go to the shopping stalls. Even Adam was eager to look at what was for sale. He knew what to do. He simply declared, "We came here first to learn more about our Indian friends. We will look at these things later. For right now, please come over with me to listen to White Eagle." Without giving time for a response, he turned and started walking towards the amphitheater, taking Rachael, Zac and Adam by surprise. They followed, still talking all the way, into the theater.

Rachael and Zac became really angry when they realized he had led them away from their bows, arrows and dresses. As the realization struck, they lashed out in anger. Rachel began, "Why are you making us come here to listen to some boring lecture about their tradition?" Zac continued the attack, "What are we doing here? We don't want to be here! This was supposed to be a family outing and fun." Adam, playing the role of elder brother, could not resist. "We are here to learn not only about their heritage but also to honor all those who have ancient traditions, like our own. So, be quiet and sit down!"

As the rabbi saw this interaction with his children, he began to chuckle. He was thinking about the passage discussing the four children in the Passover *Seder*. The wise son asks, "What are the commandments which G-d has commanded us?" He is wise because he includes himself in the group that is obliged to yearly re-tell the stories embodied in the *Seder*. On the other hand, the wicked one says, "What is this observance to you?" He excludes himself from the *Seder* ritual. The simple son asks, "What is this?" He is viewed as not very sophisticated and is to be answered in a simple and straightforward manner. Finally, the son who is unable to ask is unable to fully comprehend the magnitude of history and therefore one starts to teach this child from the beginning. And that morning, as he heard his children and thought of the four children from the *Seder*, he wanted to ask the Native American children now seated around the amphitheater how many of them were happy to be present and how many were angry that their parents made them attend.

This thought of the four children made the rabbi stop and wonder if he always saw the world through Jewish eyes. Yes, he acknowledged. Our tradition teaches us to live in this world as Jews. To remember our heritage. When a group of Jewish leaders visited with the Dali Lama, this important Buddhist leader asked the Jewish guests for suggestions on how to keep his people and their traditions intact during their exile from Tibet. One of their answers was the Passover *Seder*. This meal, with all of its rituals and foods, was used for thousands of years to remind the Jewish community of its history and its hope to someday return to Israel. The final phrase of the *Seder* is "next year in Jerusalem." Accordingly, it was suggested that the Dali Lama consider instituting some type of a ritual that embodied a teaching of Buddhism's central stories and values with the hope of the participant's eventual return to Tibet. They need to be taught, as we have been taught, to always remember who we are and where we came from. At the same time, it was important to respect and learn from other traditions. The rabbi was proud that he was open to the teachings of others and he hoped his children would have such open minds. And he hoped that this Native American elder would be able to capture his children's attention.

White Eagle wasn't that tall. His face was deeply wrinkled, giving testimony to his chronological age and suggesting a deep spiritual understanding. Initially, the rabbi was put off when White Eagle did not have a prepared text or a joke to help get the audience's attention. Rather, he started talking very simply.

He welcomed the people in a very frank and direct manner. "I would like to share some thoughts with you. Many of you think you know about Indian traditions because you have seen us on television and in the movies. First, know that much you have been taught about us is not true. And, those who make the movies have only shown you customs from my brothers who live in the Plains. Rarely have you ever seen and heard about us who lived along the Pacific Ocean. You may wonder where my large colorful headdress is. Well, not all Indians dress, live or act the same. Like many of you from different parts of the country or even from different parts of the world, your dress and manner of living might be quite different. My people use magpie tail feathers."

Pointing to the seven feathers standing straight over a white down crown, he said, "These are not as colorful as you have been taught to expect. But, these are what my people have worn in this part of the country before we were 'discovered'." He threw this word out in a tone that showed a great deal of pain and bitterness. "Please remember, we lived, worked and died here well before the Spanish and all the other explorers ever heard the earth was not flat." He then pointed to the covering around his waist. "Again, you see that I am covered by a dance skirt made of eagle down with twisted plant fiber string. This is also something that may be very different than what you expected." The rabbi honestly had expected to see a colorful headdress and hear an inspiring speaker.

White Eagle continued trying to shake the pre-conceived images that he presumed the audience might have had about Native Americans. The rabbi's first thought was that this presentation was for non-Indians. However, he quickly realized it was also addressed to the many Native Americans who perhaps had forgotten their history or were willing to accept the self-denigrating notions often created by the media. "When you hear the drums beating in a few minutes, you will notice that the beat is very different from the rhythm you have been taught by television and movies. As you listen to our Indian drums, hear not only their beat but the voices of the ancestors singing to you."

He took out a small white tube and began to blow. "This is a bird bone whistle which we use when we dance."

The rabbi was beginning to be captivated by the subtlety of his presentation and the intensity of his eyes, and found himself listening to the man's heart. He felt the living history, the passion of this teacher. This was a very special man. Then, the rabbi was startled as White Eagle completely switched topics and went into a seemingly rambling diatribe against drugs and alcohol. "Drugs are bad and can trap you. Drinking is dangerous and can destroy you. Even if your parents drink or take drugs, even if your brother drinks or takes drugs, stop! Stop! Stop!" Rabbi Daniels recalled the sign across the road to the Preservation declaring that liquor and drugs were prohibited.

The rabbi wondered where this focus on drugs was coming from. Perhaps, he mused, White Eagle was addressing the well-publicized problem of alcohol on the reservation. Or, the rabbi reflected, maybe White Eagle had made his own journey through addiction and darkness.

White Eagle continued and talked about regaining the pride of being an Indian. He reminded those present about the great culture, heritage, and history of his people and those who stripped them of their pride by calling them "savages." "Who were the savages?" he asked rhetorically. "We did not demand that those from across the ocean dress like us. We did not demand that they believe like us. We did not make them slaves. Rather, we welcomed them in peace -- and they enslaved, killed, and forced us to be like them. Who were the savages?" White Eagle stopped and looked around.

61

Rabbi Daniels knew that this last part of the speech was coming out of White Eagle's pain. The passion was deep and the rage barely hidden. He was now somewhat in awe of this man. It was as if White Eagle was growing bigger as he spoke, for he was speaking on behalf of all the Indian Nations and all the ancestors. This was a true elder. He had never met an elder before, someone who had stored within him the songs and hopes of all those who had gone before. An elder was someone who willingly lived in the way of the tradition and allowed all the stored up knowledge and hope to emerge from his very existence.

Rabbi Daniels had met many people. Some were very famous, others extraordinarily rich, and still others who were exceedingly powerful. Yet, there was a quality to White Eagle that was different and compelling. There was a glow. There are some people who seem to take away one's energy but there are a few, a very few, who give energy to others. And yet fewer who seem to be walking sources of energy. He thought of Moses. When Moses came down from Mt. Sinai carrying the second set of tablets containing the Ten Commandments after the first ones had been smashed due to the golden calf incident, the Hebrew text says that Moses had *karan*, or light, coming forth from his face. These were the incredible beams of spiritual light that came forth from Moses after his divine encounter. The light was so intense the Bible records that Moses had to wear a veil because the glow was simply too strong for other people to endure.

The rabbi knew that most non-Jews did not have this vision of Moses. They often associated Moses with horns on his head as in Michelangelo's famous sculpture. The rabbi remembered that the word *karan* could be translated as either "horns" or "beams." Unfortunately, some were influenced by Michelangelo's rendition. When the rabbi was an undergraduate student, he had volunteered to tutor math in the afternoon to a group of underprivileged elementary school students. One day, one of his favorite students started putting his hands through the rabbi's hair. When he asked him what he was doing, the youth replied, "Oh, I thought you were Jewish, I was looking for your horns." The rabbi was sad because he knew that much harm and prejudice had been caused by the choice of interpretation of the Hebrew word *karan* to mean horns rather than spiritual beams of light.

Definitely, thought the rabbi as he was listening to White Eagle, this man had beams of light coming from him that morning. There was a spiritual presence exuding from this mortal man.

The rabbi had been deep in thought when it felt like a cord yanked him back into reality. "Do you live in a tee-pee?" Zac asked. The rabbi wanted to die. White Eagle did not laugh. He looked carefully and lovingly at Zac. White Eagle began, "That is a very good question. You have probably seen many television shows depicting Indians living in tee-pees." White Eagle carefully continued as a grandfather would, explaining a confusing concept to a grandchild. "My cousins the Sioux, Crow, Cheyenne and Blackfoot were great bison hunters of the great plains of North America. They used the skins of the bison to stretch across the wooden frames to make tee-pees. We, the Antchu, who lived on the west coast near the ocean, did not hunt buffalo or bison. Rather, we used plants such as willow, bulrushes, cattails and tree bark. Our traditional homes were dome-shaped tule homes that looked more like an open umbrella planted in the ground covered with old blankets. However, I now live in a mobile trailer."

This answer both surprised the rabbi and yet was in tune with his experience at the sweat on the Owl Preservation. "It's easy and convenient. But the real reason is that I do not want to hurt mother earth and I choose to live in a way in which I do not have to cut and scar her. The earth is our mother and every time we dig into her, we hurt her, we disrupt her. Our goal is to live in harmony with her." He then looked again at Zac and in a very gentle voice added, "Thank you for asking such a good question and for coming here to learn more about the Indian culture." Zac smiled, and the rabbi was impressed with how tenderly this man had dealt with his son.

After he finished his talk, White Eagle began to leave and then, unexpectedly, turned back and walked towards the rabbi. The rabbi had been sitting and instantly stood up when he saw the spiritual leader approach. The rabbi tried to thank him for his remarks and with a flick of his hand White Eagle brushed aside the rabbi's comments.

He stated simply, "You are the rabbi who has visited the Owl Preservation." This was more of a statement than a question. "Blue Star spoke to me of you. By the way, you are the first rabbi who has ever visited our powwow or the Owl Preservation. And, you're the first rabbi I have ever met. We are both intrigued with you."

The rabbi did not know if this was a positive or a negative statement. He certainly did feel like a unique specimen that was being examined.

"Blue Star told me something else. He detected in you something that he believes will be important to the Preservation and to our people. I take his intuition very seriously and that is why I wanted to meet you. Let's walk."

Rabbi Daniels was honored, confused and curious. He looked over to see Carol talking to his children and waved to her. She understood, smiled, and nodded and began to lead the children to the booths containing the many souvenir items for sale.

The meeting with White Eagle had an unnatural feel to it. The elder was like a teacher and the rabbi was his student. White Eagle first asked the rabbi to tell him why he had really come to the powwow. The rabbi responded as if he were talking to a rabbinic master and wanted to give an honest answer. "I'm not really sure. I know that I have much to learn about life, who I am, and where I am going. I believe that there is much from the Native American tradition that will touch me and help me on this journey." White Eagle nodded.

The rabbi continued, "When I think about Judaism, I don't think about Judaism as merely a religion. Jews don't have to believe a particular set of dogma to be Jewish. As a matter of fact, one doesn't even have to believe in G-d to be considered Jewish. We are not a race because one can join us through conversion. Actually, some of our most important Jews were those

63

who chose to convert, to join the Jewish people. It feels as if we are more like a tribe."

White Eagle smiled at that point. "Yes, this feels right to me as well. Like you, we have members of our tribe who are not active, occasionally show up, or if they could, would divorce themselves totally from their Indian traditions. And yet, they are and will always be part of our tribe. While we don't exactly let people convert, we do allow some non-Indians to become sun dancers."

"Yes," the rabbi agreed. "I sat next to one of them during my sweat at the preservation."

"That was Bill," White Eagle confirmed. "I was initially against him, against anyone who was not part of our tribe taking on our traditions. Yet, he has a strong spirit, a good heart. And, it was right that Blue Star convinced me to accept him."

They walked in silence for a few moments until White Eagle said, "I find that many things I do have been challenged by others. Currently, the tribal council wants to bring a gambling casino onto the reservation. I am strongly against this because I believe that it will hurt our people, especially our young people who will be trapped within the notion that money and happiness is the same thing. The council tells me that the casino will bring a lot of money to the reservation from tourists, produce a lot of jobs, and generally help the reservation. I don't believe this. I feel that the casino will only bring disillusionment, disappointment and death. We have enough problems on the reservation, we don't need more. However, those on the council don't agree with me. They think I am being old fashioned."

Rabbi Daniels was deeply touched. This was like two equals talking to each other in painful honesty. He revealed, "As a rabbi, I am often asked for the Jewish position on such and such an issue. If what I say agrees with their preconceived notion, they are happy. If not, they will often ask me to tell them what I really believe as if my personal beliefs would be different than my philosophy as a rabbi. They don't understand that being a rabbi is not like a professional title that I can take on or off. It is who I am. They sometimes want spiritual leaders to ease their conscience by being politically expedient. But we have an obligation to the past and to the present, to follow what we believe to be the truth."

The rabbi paused, and then concluded, "There is a rabbinic saying that you might like -- 'A rabbi whom they don't want to drive out of town isn't a rabbi.'" White Eagle did not chuckle as the rabbi had expected. White Eagle remained quiet. After a moment, the rabbi continued. "Part of our role is to not make people comfortable but to challenge them. It is a hard role, but it is our path when we choose or are chosen to be spiritual teachers." They resumed walking in silence and then White Eagle sat down on a fallen log. The rabbi wanted to know about this man and so he asked, "I would like to hear your story."

White Eagle sighed. "It is a long story, but I do like sharing it and I would like you to hear it. I was born on the reservation. I can remember hating, hating, hating. My childhood was spent hating and being lost. My father taught me to hate. He could not find a job, he drank a lot and he hated his life. And I learned to despise him for hating himself. The reservation was very dirty. We knew we were Indians and we were taught we were below everyone else. If that were not enough, we had constant reminders at school of our low status. We were told we were savages. I had no idea of my culture or history."

The rabbi thought of a time when he was in his elementary classroom and the teacher, Mrs. Clark, told the class that Santa visited only good Christian children. Either she didn't know that he was Jewish, or didn't care.

"On the reservation, we had no sweat lodges or powwows where we experienced our tradition. No one on the reservation taught children or went into the schools to share our proud traditions."

White Eagle paused as if he had to gather his inner strength to continue. "This is something I bet you didn't know. According to the federal government we are not even a tribe. The Bureau of Indian Affairs has a list of 'official tribes.' If you are on the rolls of that list, you can get federal assistance and grants. If you're not listed, you just don't exist. We're not on their list. So, other tribes didn't recognize us as being 'real' Indians. How do you like that? We were nothing. We were nowhere and I was going nowhere. So, I started to do dumb things. I was no stranger to drugs and alcohol." At that moment the rabbi understood White Eagle's detour during the presentation into his impassioned appeal and attack against the use of drugs and alcohol.

"I started to get into trouble because I simply didn't care. I did some time in juvenile hall and then graduated to prison when I was convicted of armed robbery."

This elder was an ex-con, the rabbi realized. He was shocked and amazed. How did this man, who hated so much, change so that he could treat the rabbi's son so gently? He wanted to know more and White Eagle did not disappoint him.

"But, something very strange happened in prison. I was not unique, and I found that I had many companions in prison who hated as much as I did. One of those was an African-American. He actually hated even more than me. However, he changed when he became a Black Muslim in prison. For this man, becoming a member of that community also provided him with a feeling of pride. I saw this drastic change and was so intrigued that I read the story of Malcolm X. I then had a revelation that if this man could find pride through attaching himself to the Black Muslim community, perhaps I could find pride by becoming attached to my Indian heritage.

"I looked for books about Native Americans in general, and Antchu in particular. I found a lot about the Apache and other tribes, but virtually nothing about my people. I vowed that when I left prison, I would leave behind drugs and alcohol and discover who I am through learning about my people. When I finally got out of prison, I started to sit with the old men and listen to their stories. I traveled to different reservations, always looking for more information about the Antchu nation. I wrote down what I was learning and I was able to piece together much of my folklore. Suddenly, others on and off the reservation began to ask me to tell them about our tradition. I was asked to come into schools and go before certain groups to teach our ways.

"I found out that we were hunters and known as canoe makers. Sometimes we would take 40 days and sometimes even six months to build our plank canoes because we wanted to make sure they would be able to survive in the sea. Those who knew how to build our boats were part of a special brotherhood that would help each other.

"We had our own stories. As you have your story about the flood, so do we. Spotted Woodpecker went to the tallest tree as the rains fell and all the earth was covered with water. He cried out to Sun, 'Uncle, help, I am drowning!' Sun heard his cries and lowered his touch so the water began to recede. Woodpecker was warmed and then Sun threw him acorns to eat. Woodpecker picked them and was content. This is why Woodpecker still likes acorns so much to this day.

"We had stories about the stars and the making of human hands. We had such a rich culture and yet we did not know it. Without our stories, our history, we have no pride and no honor.

"I learned also that Indian labor built many of the missions and performed much of the work for the early Spanish colonies. As they needed more of my people to help them, they urged my people to leave their villages and move into the missions where they were changed - baptized into the others' religion and taught their ways. Gradually, as the missions grew, the villages withered along with our religious and social systems. However, we did get many things from the Europeans. We learned farming and masonry. We also inherited their diseases, especially measles and smallpox, which decimated our population.

"Our people, finally realizing what was happening to them, rebelled in the early 1800s. However, troops were sent in who ruthlessly smashed the rebellion."

The rabbi interjected. "I remember learning about the mission system as a young child. It was seen as very positive. We were never told about its effect on the Indians."

White Eagle stopped and looked at the rabbi. "Yes, I know how it is taught. The mission system lasted only 60 years, by which time our once proud and culturally advanced people had virtually ceased to exist. After the mission system ended, our people had no villages to return to. Many became domestic servants and cowboys. We were lost. We became afraid to admit we were Indians; we became outcasts on our own land.

"One Antchu community did manage to survive in the St. Luke's area and they eventually moved onto the reservation. I have become their teacher. Often, people of Antchu descent come to visit, to learn about themselves. They want to build a connection to the past to give them a sense of identity in the present.

"Then friends came to me and asked me to teach their children. I answered 'no.' I will teach you instead so that you can teach your children. We started having ceremonies again and created this annual powwow."

The rabbi felt overwhelmed. He began to realize that this one man, perhaps single-handedly, resurrected the Antchu culture. Based on this man's research, tenacity, and vision, the Antchu people live. Like the Biblical Ezekiel who raised warriors from the dead, White Eagle raised his tradition from the dead. He was the living book for the people. In the Jewish tradition, everyone is commanded to "write" a Torah, the scroll containing the Five Books of Moses. For many commentators, this meant that one was to live one's life so that one would be a teacher to future generations. Certainly White Eagle had written a Torah of Antchu tradition that would light the steps for many that would follow him. Here was a man who in the process of saving himself was saving his people.

White Eagle continued speaking, now about his wife Ruth. He told the rabbi how he met Ruth. "After a while, the local university asked me to give some lectures. There was one woman who stood out. She came to every lecture and always stayed after asking questions, and her name was Ruth. Our relationship grew with her increased understanding of Indian ways. This former student is now my wife. I hope you will someday meet her. Sometimes I think she knows more about Indian traditions than I do."

The rabbi was surprised when he realized Ruth had to be much younger than White Eagle and was a non-Indian, just like Carol. Curious, he thought, that these two Indian leaders would choose to marry non-Indians.

After the rabbi left White Eagle, Zac was first to assail him. He grabbed his father's hand and demanded, "I found this great bow and arrow set, come with me." Rachael, not to be outdone, was now grabbing at his second hand with a similar demand, "*Abba*, come with me first. I found a kit to make a real dress." "No!" this was Adam's voice. "I want you to see the sweatshirts for sale. They're really different. The images go all around the shirt, even on the back." By the end, each had bought some items. As his children continued to prowl the various booths, the rabbi watched the dancing with fascination. The dancers were from various tribes throughout the Pacific southwest. He enjoyed the regalia and the drums, and the motion was intoxicating. Some had multiple feathers and brightly colored clothing. Others wore no feathers and their clothing was very simple. Carol came to stand by his side; she was also enjoying the spirit.

"I can see you are enjoying this. What are you thinking?" she asked.

This is the type of question Leah would have asked. The rabbi was missing Leah. He always enjoyed being with her. If she were here now, he would have put his hand in hers and felt the subtle warmth of her body.

"These are such amazing people and yet they were not appreciated by our ancestors and they are still not appreciated today. I am both sad and happy. They have lost so much and yet look at their happiness. These are strong and proud people. I feel privileged to be here and to be learning from them," said Rabbi Daniels.

Carol replied, "You have great kids who love you very much. They like being here. Although the dance area is sacred and you cannot enter it for most of the day, there will be a time when non-dancers will be permitted to enter. It's a special feeling to dance and I hope you will stay the afternoon."

"I would love to stay, but I must perform a wedding later in the afternoon."

"Well," concluded Carol, now resigned to the rabbi's short stay, "before you leave it is important that you taste our traditional food, fry bread." She pointed to a few stalls where the rabbi could see corn being cooked over open flames, as well as other foods. However, Rabbi Daniels became aware that Blue Star and White Eagle were talking and occasionally glancing over at him. Finally, Blue Star came over and said, "We need your help," and handed Rabbi Daniels some official looking papers.

Chapter 5
The Eviction Notice

Justice, Justice shall you pursue.
Bible, Deuteronomy

The light outside Rabbi Daniel's synagogue was waning. It was now late and the tea was finished, as was the cheesecake. The rabbi had paused and was obviously tired. Ann was also ready to leave, although she was very curious about what happened next. She remembered that the rabbi had been leaving the office a little more often and he was taking a lot of phone calls from Native Americans and lawyers. She had been inquisitive at the time. And now she was about to find out what happened, but it was time to stop for the evening.

"I have a great idea. How about if we pick up where we left off over lunch tomorrow?" she offered as she began picking up the plates and cups with the rabbi. "If I remember correctly, you have, believe it or not, no lunch meeting scheduled tomorrow. And, you should take me out to appreciate all the wonderful things I do for you."

"This is not secretary appreciation week," the rabbi protested.

Ignoring the rabbi's comment, Ann asked, "So, tomorrow for lunch?"

"OK, where does my secretary want to be taken so I can show her my appreciation for how she is always bugging me?"

"As this may be my last lunch with you, since you're planning to abandon me, how about the Log Restaurant up on Route 36?"

"You've got to be kidding! That's a 25-minute ride. And do they serve anything besides deer and bear meat?"

"I know that you only eat kosher meat. They also serve great pasta with pesto. I just want us to get away from the town so we won't run into anyone from the congregation. So, don't forget, I'm your date for lunch. Don't go and make another lunch appointment."

The next morning, Ann came into the rabbi's office at 11:30 to remind him of their lunch date. She knew that once he was in his office, the phone calls never seemed to cease. He was usually on the phone, answering the numerous e-mails, and preparing for some presentation like a busy corporate executive. Maybe this is why he's been so depressed, she thought; he is trying to do everything for everyone and is getting lost.

At noon, with her red coat obviously draped over her arm as a hint, she came into his office. He was still simultaneously on both the phone and the computer. She stood in front of him, pointing to her watch. He finally put down the phone and sent an e-mail. "I have one more phone call to make," he announced as he began to dial.

"You always have one more phone call to make, but not now." With that she gently, yet quite firmly, pulled the phone from the rabbi and placed it back in its cradle. "Don't mess with me when I'm hungry. And, I want to hear the rest of the story. I don't like cliffhangers. I had a hard time sleeping last night. So, up you go."

As Rabbi Daniels reluctantly stood up, already feeling tired from the day, he shared with Ann, "You know, I was in the market yesterday morning. Judy Stevenson was behind me with someone else and started commenting on what I was buying. Some people have no boundaries, no respect. My position does put my family into a fishbowl," the rabbi concluded.

Ann was fully aware that congregants talk about seeing the rabbi at dinner or at a movie. It was strange to her that they didn't realize he was a human being who did very human things, like take his sons out to play miniature golf or go out for pizza. Congregants seemed surprised to see him doing normal things and would often judge how he was dressed and how well behaved or not his children were. She knew that Leah's clothing choices, such as wearing bright colored socks, was a little unorthodox and had been commented on by several of the women in the sisterhood. Leah was tired one night and had even fallen asleep once during her husband's sermon. That had been the talk of the community for several weeks. She understood this type of public scrutiny could get to anyone. Maybe this was another source of the rabbi's depression.

As they walked together into the parking lot, the rabbi started heading to his assigned parking spot with the sign above: RESERVED FOR RABBI DANIELS. Ann advised, "I'm driving. I want you to concentrate on telling me the story while I concentrate on driving."

They walked over to a rather new looking Lexus. The rabbi knew Ann had some money and was working more out of her desire to be of service than need. After her husband of thirty years had died and her children moved away, she had put her energy into the Synagogue. The Lexus was nicer than he expected, even with leather seats. "I think we're paying you too much," quipped the rabbi. The stare from Ann made him quickly stop this line of comments and begin the story quickly.

"Let's see, we had finished the powwow and I had those eviction papers. Oh, yes."

As Ann pulled onto Route 36, Rabbi Daniels began.

"As I read through the document, my hands actually trembled when I began to understand the import of the letter. It was from the County of Roseville, an order to fix a long list of building and safety code violations, or vacate the property within fifteen days. One piece of paper stated that they needed to leave their home, leave their land."

Ann became indignant. "They can't just tell you to get off the land in less than two weeks, can they?"

The rabbi was quiet. Ann continued, "The County can really do that?"

"Oh yes. And that day, while holding that paper, I firmly believed this was going to happen to Blue Star and his community. It was hard for me to even look at them. But I finally lifted my gaze, stared them in the eyes and slowly revealed the obvious.

"I said, this demands that you leave your trailers, build homes consistent with the building codes and install a regular sewer system within fifteen days- or leave the land."

When Blue Star asked, "What do we do?" I really didn't have an answer. I knew that even if they wanted to comply, they had no money to make the changes. I then replied, "Brother, I'm not an expert in this area and don't really know what's the best approach. Let me find an attorney who can help you. Give me a day and call me back tomorrow night, okay?"

"But you're an attorney," Ann interrupted. "Why couldn't you help him? I know, you didn't practice for that long and you don't feel that confidant." Ann spoke furiously.

"Each area of law is its own specialty with its own procedures. I don't know this area and it would have been better to find them an expert. And, there is something more, Ann. These cases can drag on for a long period of time."

"Now tell the truth! You just didn't want to be bothered!" Ann continued with a creeping bitterness in her voice.

"That's what I like about you, Ann, your calm demeanor." The rabbi made this last comment with levity in his tone in an attempt to deflect her growing irritation.

"I had to find more information. I found two legal defense organizations that help Native Americans, one in Boulder, Colorado and one in Washington, D.C. The attorneys I talked with were nice, but were too busy to help. They were already involved with lawsuits dealing with Native Americans on reservations and didn't want to fight this battle involving Indians living off the reservation."

"I don't understand. Blue Star is an American Indian and needed help. Why does it matter if he is on or off the reservation?" Ann questioned somewhat indignantly.

"I'm not really sure. Maybe they're stuck in the frame of mind that they need to defend the reservations from assimilationists. Remember, for most of our American history we tried to destroy the Native American culture because it was thought to be barbaric. It seemed our goal was to help them adopt the prevalent Christian religion. Then, as we developed more 'progressive' and 'tolerant' government policies, the protection of the reservation became the main focus. I just don't think they understood the concept that Blue Star wanted to live off the reservation and didn't want to totally assimilate."

"I finally found Marine Legal Aid which had done some work for another Native American community to stop a university that wanted to build some dorms on a burial site. Unfortunately, the court ruled in favor of the university citing a Supreme Court case. In Lang, the United States Supreme Court allowed the forestry service to build a road through a burial site."

Ann was furious. "How could they plow right through a burial ground? I thought the First Amendment protected people's religion? It's just not fair!" moaned Ann while she expertly navigated the turns as they moved higher up the mountainside. From this point, the vastness of the ocean stretched out below them and they could see the whole of St. Luke's.

The rabbi responded as if to a student, "One might think that Native American practices would be protected by the First Amendment, but they are not. I remember a comment by a leader of the Navajo Nation, which I still can recall:

74

"I still can't believe it. After all that our nation has done to its first inhabitants, I would have expected our highest court to protect them rather than to continue the persecution. Perhaps if we had a church and went there once a week they would respect us. But our church is the mountains, rivers, clouds and sky.'"

The rabbi paused. "A powerful and sad statement." He looked at Ann who quietly nodded her head.

"Anyway, Ben Goldman was the attorney with whom I was eventually connected. He was willing to review the documents and advise the Owl Preservation. It was with a great deal of relief that I faxed the documents over to his office. I immediately called Gus' tavern and left the message that I had found an attorney and Blue Star should call me the following day."

"My hero," Ann affirmed as she looked up with feigned hope spreading across her face. "Well done, you got them a lawyer."

However, at this comment, the rabbi looked away, and as if speaking to the car door, replied, "Ben Goldman called me back the following morning with some very negative information. I will never forget his phone call. I could tell from the beginning there was a problem. I'll give you the gist of the conversation. He had a strong, deep voice. 'Hello, this is Ben Goldman from the Marine Legal Aid. I received your fax. I won't waste time being nice. If they do live in mobile trailers and use pit toilets, then they are in violation of county building and health codes. The county has the authority to kick them off the land. However, I am sure I can contact the county and get your friends an extension of time to move out. Probably I can get them an additional month's time.'"

The rabbi paused. Ann glanced at the rabbi, who said, "I was so stunned, I literally could not speak. I realized the attorney was telling me that Blue Star and his community would have to move off the land. When I asked him where would they go, do you know what he answered me? He calmly replied, 'Back to the reservation, of course.' He even told me to let them go back and apply for grants to make the necessary repairs and then return to the land in three or four years. I told him that if they left the land, they would probably never return. I decided right then and told him I would take over the case."

A broad smile crept over Ann's face. "I thought that you, a busy high profile rabbi, were too important to be bothered!"

The rabbi smiled back and winked. "I really had no choice. You see, in American law one has no duty to come to the rescue of someone drowning. In Jewish law, in Leviticus, we are commanded to 'not stand idly by the blood of your neighbor.' In other words, I had to help my newly found brother and community."

Ann just smiled. "So what did you do, Mr. Lawyer-slash-Rabbi?"

The rabbi's joyous mood shifted somewhat as he spoke. "There is an old legal adage. When the facts are on your side, you argue the facts. When the law is on your side, you argue the law. When neither is on your side, you pound the table and you scream. I began to scream."

"Funny," quipped Ann. "I always scream when the facts are on my side." She looked at the rabbi and shook her head. "I'm afraid I can't see you yelling."

"Ask my kids. I yell," he confessed. "But not too often," he added. "I knew we had to be creative and find a political solution rather than a legal one. The county supervisors make the regulations, which the building and health officers enforce. They can change the regulations or find ways around them. So, I had to find a way to get to the supervisors.

"When I was in rabbinical school, one of my fellow students was Judy Silver who became a rabbi to a congregation located near the county offices. On a hunch, I contacted her. I told her the situation and she called me back.

"She addressed me by my first name when she picked up the phone. 'Elijah, you were always lucky and you are lucky again. The most supportive supervisor is Kate O'Brien and she happens to be the supervisor for the district where your friends are located. When you call, you won't get to her directly. Ask for her aide, Tom Hernandez. He's a good man. Give him the facts and if he can help, he will. Best of luck!'"

Ann broke in, "Before you continue, and I know you're into the story, but I do have a question about female rabbis. Can I ask a short question?"

"Ann, your questions are rarely short."

"I know there are more women rabbis today than ever before. And, that there were a few women rabbis who also applied for this position when you did. I heard some of the members of the search committee debating if the congregation would be open to a woman rabbi. How accepted are these rabbis?"

"Ann, I wish I could categorically tell you there were no problems. Change is difficult; nevertheless, there is progress. Over half the students in the liberal rabbinical schools are women and some of the more major congregations are finally willing to interview and hire women. Frankly, I like having female colleagues. They often see things that I have been blind to. Female rabbis have written some great commentaries and shown a different and fascinating perspective. They are in many ways my teachers and they have helped all of us, men and women, take issues of rabbinic sanity more seriously."

Rabbi Daniels looked at this watch, "Now, may I get on with the story?" Taking silence as assent, the rabbi continued, "When I phoned, I was put through quickly to Mr. Hernandez. And true to what I was told by my friend, he listened very carefully and asked a few questions. He then told me he could look into the matter and get back to me. However, I reminded him these people had a fifteen-day-no, then it was more like a ten day-order to get off the land. Hernandez simply replied don't worry and told me the order was on hold. I asked him if I had his word on that. 'You have my word,' Mr. Hernandez told me.

"That night when Blue Star called from Gus' tavern, I told him we lost our attorney and what I had done. He shared an amazing thing with me.

'Brother, we had a special sweat today and were praying. In my prayers, I felt that you were the one who would represent us.'"

"How did that make you feel?" Ann inquired as she made a careful left turn off the main highway onto a smaller road.

"I felt both burdened and afraid that I could not live up to their expectations. And, I felt perhaps it was destined that I would represent them."

"Now this is interesting. You really believe in this destiny thing? Is that common among rabbis?"

"No, not really. But, it certainly makes life more interesting. Rather than just seeing life as random events, I look for the connections. I believe that we live in a world filled with divine opportunities, which we can choose to follow or ignore. There is so much we don't understand that I have consciously chosen to seek divine guidance. It makes me more of a seeker than just a traveler."

Ann reduced the car's speed significantly because of the basketball-sized potholes. A hummingbird caught both their attention. The Lilliputian, a scarlet-throated bird, was looking in, poised in mid-flight as if she were listening in through the open window of the car.

The rabbi looked at the bird as well. "Tom was true to his word. He called back the next day and informed me that in ten days there would be a meeting at the county offices and I should be there, along with a few representatives from the Owl Preservation. He stressed that Ms. O'Brien would like to help but would need something beyond their good will to overrule the building and health officers."

"I immediately called Gus' and left an urgent message for Blue Star to call a meeting at my house. Two nights later, Blue Star, Carol and Bill Harris sat in my living room. Bill was a tall man with gray hair. He stood straight and seemed to be in great condition. He worked for the Forest Service and was meeting with us in an unofficial capacity"

Ann took one hand off the wheel and raised her hand as if in school to get the rabbi's attention. "Sorry for all the questions, but I've got another one. How'd you feel having Blue Star and Carol at your home? After all, it's big, beautifully done and expensive. You've described the preservation as being really poor. Did you think about this during your meeting?"

"Yes, I felt pretty awkward. My house has three bathrooms; we have two televisions, nice carpets and large rooms. And Brenda lives with us to take care of the kids. I was very self- conscious of my opulence. Here I am, a spiritual leader, yet I'm surrounded by many luxurious material things."

Ann was satisfied with the answer and moved on to a different topic. "So, what was your political strategy?"

"We decided we wanted to show the people at the meeting why the preservation was so important. So, we were going to get letters of support from the schools that visited, veterans who came for healing ceremonies, people needing our support during vision quests. Moreover, Bill from the Forest Service volunteered to get a strong letter of support from his superiors mentioning all the help provided by Blue Star to identify and protect Native American sites in the national forests."

The rabbi had been so focused on his story that as he looked around he asked, "How much longer to this famous restaurant you mentioned? It seems like we've been driving for awhile."

Ann answered, "I think I turned off too soon. I don't remember these large potholes or this dirt road. I'm going to turn around." As if to emphasize that something was wrong, the silver Lexus made a wheezing sound like an emphysema patient gasping for air. Ann and the rabbi looked at each other and shrugged. The car continued down the dirt road normally, which now had become quite narrow. "Well, I guess even thirty thousand dollars of high-tech engineering is entitled to an occasional sneeze," joked the rabbi.

A minute later the car wheezed and died. Ann wrestled with the car as the power steering went out and she tried to maneuver it to a shoulder. The dirt road afforded nothing on its borders but a weed-infested drainage ditch. Ann turned the key that connected her with the high tech car and the powerful engine responded by making a simple clicking sound.

"What's a clicking sound mean?" asked the rabbi.

"I'd guess it means we'll be walking back to town, unless you know something about car repair."

"I imagine I know as much as you."

"Wonderful, I know nothing."

"That's what I mean. But unlike you, I'm plugged into the twenty-first century. I have a cell phone that can help me locate people who can get me any help I want, anywhere in the world," the rabbi declared with pride. He reached for his phone only to find an empty place where the twenty-first century should have been.

"Oh no. I left it on my desk."

"Well, the nineteenth century wasn't so bad. People walked everywhere back then. It gave them healthy appetites and they could eat more and gain less than people with cars who never walk."

The rabbi was straining at the lock on the car.

Ann pushed a button and all the car doors unlocked with a pronounced chunking sound. They exited the car. The rabbi popped the hood and stared at what appeared to be an infinite galaxy of wires, tubes and hoses.

"Is there any engine under there?" asked Ann.

"I think so." He examined the workings of her esteemed vehicle more carefully for a few minutes, then abruptly closed the hood. "Somebody will come along and give us a ride," he concluded with confidence.

"You don't seem very upset."

"I've decided to relax. On my better days, I can be quite spiritual. So, I'm viewing this as a holy adventure. Life is a mystical journey where you don't always know where you're going to end up. So, we ended up here. I wonder for what reason? And to be honest, as I often say, the journey itself is more important than its destination." He grabbed a sign supplied by the Auto Club from Ann's trunk that read 'I need assistance' and placed it in the window. He switched on her four way flashers and jumped over the drainage ditch with an impressive leap. "Let's enjoy the scenery."

Ann also jumped over the ditch with the help of a little run first. For a woman of her age she was quite agile. The Rabbi knew she liked to take hikes and loved nature. She picked what appeared to be a tiny hot pink berry. She scraped off the pink crust and scratched the black nugget with her thumb. She held it up to the rabbi's nose.

"Pepper?" he inquired, and then sneezed. "I never knew. Here we have pepper trees right across from our house, and we buy pepper at the supermarket."

"Probably imported from another state or country," added Ann.

"We're all out of touch with the earth," the rabbi acknowledged. "Most kids would prefer to play electronic games than take a hike," he added.

"Shouldn't we stand by the car?" asked Ann.

"Why? We're blocking the road," the rabbi concluded. He walked a few yards to a streambed. Ann joined him. On both sides large green-leafy oak trees, sycamores, and poison oak. The rabbi stopped, standing precariously on top of some smooth stones in the middle of the path, a spot that was usually under rushing water in rainy seasons. "It feels great to be down here. I love the blessing of seeing a rainbow or experiencing an earthquake. When I become overwhelmed by the beauty of nature, I say a blessing." The rabbi paused, looked around at the leaves of the tress, the clear sky, and the brown of the earth and shouted, "Blessed is the Source of creation who has created all."

Ann smiled and continued a little further until she found a boulder in the riverbank. She climbed onto the boulder and reclined back.

"Is that comfortable?" the rabbi asked. He remembered the Biblical Jacob who had his dream of a ladder to heaven, sleeping on a pile of stones. That never seemed very comfortable to him.

"My favorite place to sit is on boulders," she shared. "They do wonderful things to your body. They're full of healing magic." The rabbi was seeing a side of Ann that he had never imagined. She seemed relaxed and happy in nature.

The rabbi noticed that Ann's pant legs were already patched with dirt from the boulder she was sitting on. He looked at his grey suit pants. He only had two suits. Yet the boulder was appealing. He used a handkerchief to dust off an area on the rock. He sat, a little stiffly.

"Lay back," instructed Ann.

He took off his jacket and carefully folded it inside to keep it from getting dirty and placed it warily on another boulder. He reclined, slowly lowering his back onto the surface of the rock. The stone was warm from the sun. It didn't feel as hard as it looked. There was an illusion of softness in fact.

He looked up at the sky through the pepper tree leaves. He could discern dozens of smells; he could put a name to only a few. "We might as well continue the story, don't you think?" he asked.

"Good idea," said Ann, her eyes shut. She was obviously enjoying the sunshine of the afternoon.

"Let's see, I was telling you about our strategy for the preservation. Well, we put together booklets with all the letters of recommendations, especially from the Forest Service, created a history of the preservation, and provided additional information. Then came the day of the actual meeting."

Rabbi Daniels was dressed in a grey, three-piece pinstripe suit and a vest with a red power tie. He drove up in his black sports car to the St. Luke's county offices.

On the one hand, he looked like a lawyer and had even found his old grey leather briefcase, appropriately worn on the edges, for the occasion. On the other hand, he didn't know many lawyers who also wore a *kippah*. He also didn't know a lot of rabbis with black sports cars.

Just as planned, and somewhat to the rabbi's surprise, Blue Star drove up on time in a battered and quite dirty white VW van with a spare tire attached to its front. He was dressed in a blue shirt, white pants, a red sash, a red bandanna, and a string of turquoise beads around his neck. Carol came out of the passenger side all in white except for one brown bead held in place by a black leather string around her neck. And then, to the rabbi's utter admiration, White Eagle slowly emerged from the now open sliding side door of the van. He was dressed just as he was at the powwow-the feathers on top, bare-chested with the magpie skirt. They greeted each other with warm hugs and greetings of "brother." As they began walking towards the tall, stark, concrete office building, the rabbi looked over at White Eagle and imagined the Antchu nation walking with this man.

This strange group stopped in the courtyard before entering the now increasingly imposing building with its large glass windows, and the rabbi announced to everyone, "Let's make sure we are prepared. Carol, did you bring copies of the booklets with all the support letters?" Carol nodded. "Alright, I don't know exactly how this is going to go. I might ask each of you to make a statement or respond to questions." As he continued, the rabbi noticed that White Eagle was barely paying attention and had taken out a bundle of white sage.

Finally, when the rabbi had stopped talking, White Eagle looked at him and said, "Relax. You've done all that you could do. Now, we need to prepare our way." With that he lit the sage and let it catch on fire for a few moments and then blew it out. Then White Eagle blew it again to increase the smoke as he began a chant that grew in intensity so that it was echoing off of the concrete building. The rabbi began thinking of the Biblical trumpets blasting the walls down around Jericho. White Eagle took the sage and carefully circled Carol, fanning it with an eagle feather that he had brought. Carol made sure to carefully lift her feet. Carol took the sage and eagle feather from Blue Star and fanned the sage as she circled White Eagle. Rabbi Daniels was honored when White Eagle circled him with the sage. The rabbi even remembered to carefully lift his feet. He was taken by surprise when he was asked to sage around Blue Star. The rabbi had presumed that he would not be allowed to perform this ceremony. He hoped he was doing it right as he fanned the eagle feather. The rabbi knew they needed all the divine help they could get. He glanced up and could see groups of people in many of the windows looking down. He wondered what they were thinking. He was nervous and felt like a David about to fight Goliath. He only hoped that his aim would be as good.

White Eagle must have sensed the rabbi's discomfort and grabbed the rabbi. White Eagle's grip was surprisingly strong in spite of his age. The elder looked at the rabbi and remarked, "Thank you for helping us."

The rabbi replied, "I hope that I can do a good job."

White Eagle answered in a very calm voice, "You will."

They were carefully checked by the security officers, directed to an elevator and told to go to a conference room on the third floor. The room was as stark as the building. No decorations, no plants, and no windows. There were fifteen chairs with green padding around a long rectangular dark wooden table. The room was not cheerful. And it was empty. They were the first to arrive and started to sit together on one side of the table when the rabbi stopped them and instructed, "I want all of us to space out around the table, don't sit together. When people come in, welcome them and ask them who they are and what they do. I want to change the energy so it's not us against them but one large group working together." Carol smiled at this and moved to the other side of the table. Blue Star and White Eagle took opposite corners.

It was funny to watch the obvious confusion on the faces of the various public officials as they entered. They did not know where to sit and were visibly uncomfortable being forced to sit next to the others. The rabbi had used this technique when doing mediations just to try and change the natural tendencies to see everything as an adversarial contest with winners and losers.

He looked at each person as they entered and tried to connect their name with their position. The first person to enter and the most uncomfortable was Burt Steel. He was the investigator who had sent the letter giving Blue Star fifteen days. He had a very short haircut, stood erect, and dressed in a blue power suit, a white shirt and a red tie. The rabbi bet that Burt had been in the military, probably the Marines. The two people from the building and safety office were dressed in a more casual manner, white shirts and ties. The two representatives from the health and safety office were also less formal. When they sat down, they each gave Carol, White Eagle, Blue Star and the rabbi their business cards. White Eagle took the four crisp white cards and placed them end-to-end in front of him. He had no pocket to put these cards into and had no cards to give back. Rabbi Daniels was the only one with a card. All he had were cards from the synagogue that would quickly dispel the masquerade of being a powerful, no-nonsense attorney. He thought of not passing his out but thought better. He hesitantly passed them out and was rewarded with quick glances as they realized he was not a normal attorney. The rabbi couldn't initially tell if this was a good or a bad thing. He soon found out.

Burt looked at the card carefully and asked with a disappointed voice, "I thought you were a lawyer, not a rabbi."

"Oh, I am a lawyer also." Rabbi Daniels replied a little too quickly and loudly, displaying his own level of discomfort.

As directed, Carol attempted to engage in conversation with those around her only to be greeted by a wall of silence. Everyone was quiet, yet expectant. Tom Hernandez, with a blue blazer, white shirt and blue tie, walked in and worked the room by shaking everyone's hand. He had a broad, sincere smile, hiding any emotions. He was a slick politician who was going to stay very neutral until he knew how this was going to turn out. And then the supervisor Kate O'Brien came in. She had on a striking red dress that set off her gray hair. It was clear that she did not like chitchat. She held their future in her hands and the rabbi immediately liked her very intelligent and clear brown eyes.

She began the meeting by asking for everyone's name and position, which she carefully wrote down. Without preliminaries she began, "Mr. Steel, would you please begin."

Burt Steel took out a folder and started by saying, "While this property is called a 'preservation,' it is not a reservation. It is private property and thus not entitled to the special rules governing reservations. On reservations, I am told, they can do pretty much what they want. However, the Owl Preservation is private land. As such, it is under the jurisdiction of this county and subject to all of the rules and regulations we apply to any other property." He then listed the various infractions; unsafe mobile trailers, no foundations, no running water, pit toilets. After each infraction he cited the appropriate code section. He was very efficient. When he had finished, the supervisor turned to Rabbi Daniels.

"Rabbi, it is my understanding that you are representing this group. Would you like to speak?"

The rabbi nodded to Carol who quickly passed out the packets they had prepared. He went over the material and was very pleased to see everyone thumb through the twenty pages of letters of support. They were obviously impressed.

However, Burt Steel quickly spoke up, "I am happy that many groups, even the park service, like what you are doing. But, the fact remains that you are in violation of numerous building, safety and health codes."

The Rabbi wasn't sure Ann was hearing his story since her eyes were closed as she was stretched out on the boulder. And then she said unexpectedly, her eyes now open, "Come on, Rabbi, didn't you want to hit the guy?"

"Honestly, no. I really do try to see everyone as a divine messenger, even those I may not like."

"Really!" shouted Ann.

"Really," answered the rabbi. After a pause, he added, "However, I did wish a lightning bolt would hit him."

"Good, I was about to think that you were superhuman. What happened next?"

"I needed time to get a better sense of the proceedings and the supervisor. So I began, 'Native Americans have not been provided protection...'"

The rabbi was cut short by the supervisor. "Rabbi, we are not here to discuss past abuses towards Native Americans."

He had expected Burt, not the supervisor, to attempt to steer the conversation. This made him a little concerned, but it could be a good opening. The rabbi knew the supervisor had been a lawyer and the legal debate could be energizing.

"No, Madam Supervisor, I am discussing the First Amendment and, under the Sherbet and Yorder decisions, governments and their agencies are required to make reasonable accommodations when rules come into conflict with serious religious activities. For example, a Sikh is required under his religious belief to wear a special knife called a Capon. A Sikh child attending a public school was told that the school policy prohibited knives for very obvious reasons. However, the court helped the school to understand that it had a duty to try to accommodate this child's religious belief."

Burt couldn't contain himself and blurted, "Don't tell me they allowed the kid to wear his knife and endanger the other kids?"

The rabbi waited for the discomfort of Burt's outburst to settle, and then purposely facing the supervisor he continued "No, the court asked if the knife was sewn in so tightly that it could not be removed, would this not serve both the child's religious needs as well as take care of the valid concerns of the school?"

He saw what he had hoped to see-a small smile cross the supervisor's face, "What a brilliant solution," offered Supervisor O'Brien.

Rabbi Daniels had his opening. "All we are asking is for the building, safety and health offices to be willing to look at reasonable accommodations."

The supervisor looked at Burt for a response, who was not at a loss for something to say. "Madam Supervisor, what is so religious about living in ugly mobile homes that may fall over during an earthquake?"

The rabbi responded by pointing out the preservation is surrounded on three sides by a national park. Therefore, no one is going to be worried about their land values going down because of being next to a mobile home. Then he talked about how the community did not want to create buildings that would hurt mother earth. "The Indians who traveled through Yosemite National Park for thousands of years had never hurt the land, leaving only grinding holes in some of the rocks as opposed to all the roads, buildings and campsites that have been erected recently. In a very similar way, those who live on the Owl Preservation simply want to erect shelters that will protect them but not damage mother earth. If the building concerns were to prevent these homes from tipping over during an earthquake, perhaps allowing for concrete reinforcements above ground that do not have to be dug into the earth would be a good accommodation."

Burt would not give up and decided to weigh in on the legal discussion. "But is this a religious issue or simply a cultural issue which is not protected by the First Amendment?"

Before the rabbi could respond, White Eagle raised his hand. It was not as if he was asking for permission to speak. Rather, his gesture was like a tall tree saying to a passing traveler, look at me, I have something to teach you that is ancient and powerful. "Madam Supervisor," he began, "I am not a lawyer and I really do not understand the issue of religion versus culture. However, if we were discussing a church or a synagogue, you would know how to protect it with your laws. But our church is the sky and the river and the land. We ask you to please respect our way of life as well." His voice was so gentle, yet it was ageless and full of power.

Ann's eyes were wide open. She was carefully listening to the rabbi.

"That was a good response. How was it received?" Ann asked.

"Everyone nodded, except guess who?" replied the rabbi.

"Burt then asked, 'What about pit toilets? Allowing human waste into the ground can affect local ground water and is very dangerous. It is simply unsanitary. Why can't you put in a septic system?'"

Burt knew the cost of putting in a septic system was far beyond the means of those living on the preservation. The rabbi was thinking of a clever response when Carol spoke.

"Your codes only allow for two options: we can be hooked up to a main sewer system which would mean laying around thirty miles of pipe or put in a septic system that requires a great deal of running water. Water, for us, is a ritual substance. We honor water and do not want to desecrate it with human waste. I was Catholic, and as I presume you know, holy water is treated very carefully. For us, all water is holy and we do not urinate in sacred water. If pit toilets are not safe, we can use composting or other systems that do not use water."

Ann loved this comment. "I like this Carol. But I don't understand her being Catholic and marrying a Native American. I wonder what her beliefs are now."

"Carol is an amazing person who seems to have put the two traditions together. I don't fully understand it. I also wondered how she would describe her religious beliefs now. I'll make a mental note to ask her later. I do know that the supervisor was touched by Carol's comment.

Burt was now becoming a little desperate and had one more thing to say -- and it proved to be the highlight of the meeting.

Mr. Steel picked up the papers in front of him and purposely flipped through them. He then looked up. "I am also concerned about their unhealthy use of gray water. They take showers or wash dishes and save the water in buckets. They then take this dirty water and use it to water plants. This is also against our health codes."

The rabbi was about to frame an answer when the supervisor spoke up. "Excuse me, Mr. Steel, but I seem to remember that when people were painting their lawns green with a vegetable dye three years ago during our long drought, you went on the radio and our local television stations proposing that residents place buckets in their showers and use that water to water their plants. It seems to me that if this procedure was safe for us then, it is safe for them now."

The blood rushed from Burt Steel's face. It was priceless. The rabbi had a hard time stopping himself from laughing. Burt was about to say something in his defense, but the supervisor silenced him with a look that would have stopped a train in its tracks.

She turned to Rabbi Daniels. "Well, Rabbi, what do you propose? Your people are in violation. I may want to help, but I'm not sure what I can do."

Rabbi Daniels reached his arms to the sky and stretched his legs; the boulder was now not so comfortable.

"Sometimes I gamble."

"You don't go to Vegas, do you, Rabbi?" Ann asked.

"Yes, once every two years I go with my brother. Leah hated Vegas and wouldn't set foot there. It's fun for a short time. I have a system that lets me lose over a longer period of time. To be honest, I actually enjoyed the time just walking around with my brother more than the gambling."

Smiling, she asked, "Do you wear your *kippah* when you are at the blackjack tables?"

Sheepishly he said, "No, I have a leather cowboy hat. Anyway, I bet you can't guess what I did next at the hearing?"

"You told a story," Ann smirked.

"You're right," the rabbi laughed.

"I had waited and now it was my time to gamble. Everything would depend on whether I was reading the supervisor's temperament correctly."

"Madam Supervisor, may I tell you a children's story?" Rabbi Daniels offered with his eyes fixed on the supervisor.

"Just keep it short and it better help us come to some resolution," she replied.

"Sukkot is a Jewish holiday during which we build makeshift structures outside our homes to observe this week long festival. I put palm branches on top of mine. We eat and sometimes sleep in this structure. There are many reasons for building a *Sukkah*; one of them is to remind us that physical structures are not as important as spiritual connections.

"Well, there is a story of an old man who lived in a tall apartment building. He gathered wooden doors, old crates, and other items, and piece by piece carried them up to the roof of this grand apartment building. He even brought palm branches to the roof. The manager kept seeing this man taking these items into the apartment building. This manager finally goes up to the roof and sees this flimsy structure and demands that this thing be taken down immediately. When the man refuses, the manager takes him to court.

"The judge listened to the man explain why he built the *Sukkah* and the manager explained that it was against the apartment's policies. The judge looked at the man who built the *Sukkah* and ruled that he had violated the policies of the apartment building, not to mention the county's building ordinances." The rabbi could tell that the supervisor's patience was waning, but he thought it could still work. He continued the story. "The judge then said to the man, 'I am sorry, but you must take down your structure.'" The rabbi paused for great effect and continued, "And I am giving you only ten days to comply with this order. The manager was outraged and the old man was first confused, but then smiled. The old man then stared at the judge and said, 'May G d bless you.'"

Rabbi Daniels then stopped, and whispered a silent prayer.

The supervisor looked bewildered. The rabbi held his breath. A few seconds passed in anguish and then she turned to Mr. Steel. "I see here a great deal of room for further discussion and I will presume that you will work out some form of accommodation. There is therefore no need for this order to vacate the land.

The order is cancelled." She smiled at the rabbi and left the room. Mr. Hernandez, who was walking behind the supervisor, stopped and came over to Rabbi Daniels. He shook the rabbi's hand and confided, "Very creative and well done."

The rabbi stood up and shook hands graciously with all those at the meeting, including Burt, and told the bewildered Blue Star, Carol and White Eagle they should go back to their cars.

Once outside in front of their cars, they all gathered around the rabbi.

"What the heck happened in there?" Blue Star asked. "You told that cute story, which I didn't really follow, and then we were leaving."

Rabbi Daniels was smiling with relief. "The supervisor told Burt that he had to find some way to accommodate the Owl Preservation. She wants you to stay on the land."

"Wait," Blue Star interjected, "what happens if he finds no way to let us stay? He doesn't seem like the accommodating type."

"The supervisor was not giving him a choice. She was ordering him to find an accommodation. There is no order to vacate, it is cancelled. It is like the story of the *Sukkah*; he had all the time he needed for his ritual needs. She is giving you all the time you need, which I guess will be many years. You are on the back burner as far as the county is concerned and Burt has been told to let you go."

Ann, now fully sitting up and smiling, concluded, "You won without going to court. Well done. You seem quite proud; I'm impressed with how you manipulated that hearing to allow Blue Star to stay on the land. You're a better lawyer than you let on. But... don't you think that what you did was slightly unethical?"

The rabbi chuckled. "You are like the Rambam."

"Who? I don't think I've met him."

"Well, that would be difficult unless you believed in channeling. Rambam, also called Maimonides, was a doctor to the royal household in Egypt in the last part of the 12th century. He is also considered our greatest legal scholar. He didn't like lawyers very much and called them *orech din* - those who manipulate the law."

"He and Shakespeare would get along."

"While I do generally agree with the Rambam, there is another principle that I take very seriously: '*Tzedek, tzedek, terdoff* - Justice, justice, you shall pursue.' I believe that our Native American brothers and sisters have been stripped of justice so often that I wanted to help them get a little justice. Ann, please understand I am selective as to the cases I am willing to become involved with. And, I am in turmoil about becoming involved with this murder case."

Ann rolled lazily over on her side and looked at the rabbi. He was sitting up stiffly.

"How often do you get the opportunity to really relax?" asked Ann, now playing the role of therapist. "Truly, deeply relax?"

"Relax?" asked the rabbi as if it was a foreign concept.

"It is good to see you outside of your office. You seem lighter."

Rabbi Daniels jokingly looked down and held his forty-plus stomach that was beginning to intrude over his belt. "You really think so?"

"It is no joke. I'm an old lady," she began, "and time goes fast. Don't be in such a rush." A small tear escaped her eye. "Your children grow up fast and your loved ones die. You talk about this all the time from the pulpit and yet you've become a model of just one more burned out professional. I see how your kids are hungry for your attention, for your time. In a way, you're a hypocrite."

Both were silent.

Ann had gotten up and walked a little ways into the trees. The rabbi presumed she wanted to be alone for a while and he certainly wanted to think about what she had shared.

A few minutes later, Ann called softly, "Over here, Rabbi, behind the oak grove. I want to show you something."

The rabbi walked through a small cluster of snarling oaks, bending low to avoid the giant branches suspended near to the leafy covered earth. He came immediately into a clearing. Ann was standing on a circle of stones that formed a fountain ten feet across. Behind her was a crumbling stucco building. It was surrounded by un-manicured palm trees, bloated trees with full skirts of brown fronds sitting plump underneath the green branches ruffling in the late afternoon breeze.

"What is that?" questioned the rabbi.

"It's an old retreat house. The De la Guerra, I think. There was a vote a while back for money to restore it. I think it failed. Too much politics. They're just going to let this place be forgotten. It was on the path between the mission in Santa Barbara and ours. As you know, missions were built a day's walk from each other. This was a small resting place because when the weather was bad on the mountain path they could find shelter here. This was also used to proselytizing the Antchu people. When they were debating the future of this place, it came up that it was probably built on an Antchu burial site. People were pretty upset this retreat house might have been built over a burial ground. Some wanted it restored as a historical landmark, some wanted it torn down, so they decided to do nothing."

The door to the religious structure was missing as were the windows and part of the roof. The rabbi walked up the steps, formal stone steps now soft from a thick carpet of leaves. He looked inside. Several deteriorated pews were still lined up and there was a back room for the priests to eat and sleep.

"Hardly room for more than forty people," he concluded, and returned to Ann.

She was standing in a circle of small boulders the size of basketballs, fifteen feet across. She was examining the stones that created the circle. "These are full of lines, like veins. It's as though they're alive," she observed.

"Yes," he responded. The rabbi thought about the ritual dance area at the powwow and felt this may be a sacred area. They gazed at the stones for several minutes.

They both heard the honking at the same time and rushed back to Ann's car. There was a man waving at them. As the rabbi approached, he sighed, "Oy..." It was Sam Schwartz, a congregant.

Chapter 6
Prison

A prisoner cannot free himself.
Talmud

"The rumors have started. Good ones for me in that I'm still attractive to a younger man. Bad ones for you, that you're hot for an older woman. I think I'll string up Sam by his thumbs. Want to join me?" Ann inquired with a hint of real venom in her voice.

Rabbi Daniels had been buried in a book on Jewish bioethics. He was preparing for a discussion on the Jewish views of abortion and a lunch he had for interested members once a month. Most think the Jewish view is a straight pro-choice position when it is in fact a pro-life; but the focus is on the mother's life as having priority. With Roe v. Wade always coming up in the news for one reason or another, he thought this would be an interesting topic. He put the book down on his desk and looking up revealed, "Leah would have thought this whole thing was funny. You know, I think she would have given me permission to have an affair with you if I wished. She knew I wouldn't ever violate our marriage. We totally trusted each other."

Ann always felt a little uncomfortable when the rabbi brought up Leah's name. She was also strangely aware that he didn't think that she could have made him consider breaking his vows. She still considered herself striking, perhaps a little overweight, but not bad. "I really wouldn't be worried about the rumors. People just like to talk and no one is taking it seriously."

"Oh, I'm not worried about that rumor. How are the rumors doing about my leaving?"

"I think the one about us together in the mountains has taken over. Are you still thinking of leaving?"

"I love helping people, teaching our tradition and creating spiritual moments. Have you ever been in a crowd and felt alone? That's how I sometimes feel. I want to take a path that is as rocky and dry as that waterbed that we were on and also as uncertain to the depths of my core. Yet, those around me want to take a paved straight road to a known and safe destination."

Ann could not keep some concern out of her voice. "What will you do?"

"I'm not sure. Maybe I'll just drive back up to the mountains, find that road and take more walks. Those stones up there have haunted me lately. I remember going to a concentration camp outside of Berlin called Sachsenhausen. I put stones on some of the markers where people were murdered to say that I, that we, won't forget." The rabbi suddenly became aware of how open he was becoming.

He paused for a minute, looking at the ceiling. "I'm also thinking about White Eagle. I really don't want to get involved. I can't do anything and whatever I do will be seen by someone as not being appropriate."

Ann was obviously not happy with what she was hearing. "You called him 'brother!' How can you not at least talk with him? You'd visit a congregant in jail even if he had committed murder. You don't have to absolve his action, but can you give him some comfort? You know all that. So, why are you stalling about visiting White Eagle?"

"Maybe because I can't believe and don't want to believe he would do something like this. It is as if the sky had lost all of its stars and is a solid shade of black. If a man like White Eagle could kill his wife, all of us are animals with only a very, very thin veneer of civility. I saw him as a spiritual teacher. And now he's a murderer. What does that mean? That you can't trust anyone. You never know who someone really is. I thought I knew him. I thought I could tell who the good guys were. I liked him. I trusted him. And now..."

Ann interrupted, "And now you know that people are complex and human. You know what I can't comprehend? For such a smart man you are really stupid. You think you can understand and make sense of everything. EXCUSE ME, you can't! You are not that smart and life has a way of breaking apart your organized world. And, didn't you quote in last week's sermon the old Jewish saying, 'If not now, when?' Grow up and go see White Eagle this weekend. Then, come back and tell me about it. There is still more wine and cheesecake. By the way, you still owe me a lunch and you can drive next time." Without waiting for a response, she turned on her heels and walked out of his office.

When Monday came, Rabbi Daniels returned in the afternoon after a few morning meetings and his lunch program on abortion. He stopped by Ann's desk and whispered, "We need to have a little chat with cheesecake and wine. How about 5:30?"

Smiling, Ann said, "The rumors will begin again. I also don't know what we have left in the refrigerator from this week's events."

It was closer to 6:30 when the rabbi emerged from his office with a Bar Mitzvah student and told Mr. Snyder that his son, Adam, had done a beautiful job on his speech. The father beamed as the rabbi reminded Adam, "You only have two more weeks before your Bar Mitzvah. Please make those few changes we discussed and I'll see you next week. You're really doing well and I'm proud to have the honor to officiate at your Bar Mitzvah."

After the Snyders walked out of the synagogue, Ann came out of her office.

"You really do love doing Bar Mitzvahs and helping kids. You are a good rabbi. Tell me, what do you like the most about being a rabbi?"

"Why do you want to know? Are you my therapist?" he asked in a mock tone of indignation.

Ann leaned against the hallway outside the rabbi's study that was filled with rows of simple black-framed pictures of classes that had graduated from the Temple's religious school. These pictures were the visual history of the Temple showing all the previous rabbis, cantors and educators who had stood next to all those students. Ann noticed the newest photo showed Rabbi Daniels and fifteen tenth graders standing outside in front of the synagogue's entrance. The graduates were all wearing white robes for their confirmation service and he was draped in a large blue and yellow striped *tallit* that she knew had been woven by Leah. She perceived sadness in his eyes, but there was something else-resolve. So here was Rabbi Daniels, the latest link of the unbroken chain, not only of this religious community but of the Jewish people. And it was obvious to her he was proud of the role he was playing in his people's history. That was it, she thought, he really cared and understood that what he was doing was important and mattered. If she could only help him to better appreciate these moments, maybe she could get him to stay, to be around so there would be more pictures of him on the wall surrounded by his students.

Rabbi Daniels was now also leaning against the wall in the hallway, gazing at Ann. He had crossed his arms. "I like making a positive difference and being invited into people's lives at times of celebration and tragedy. When I can make a connection for them to G-d, to each other, to previous generations, that is something special. It gives me hope that maybe what I am doing makes sense, that the world makes sense, and that I make sense. Come on, let's get some food."

Rabbi Daniels began to walk towards the kitchen and Ann followed. This time the kitchen was not empty as several Hadassah women were busy preparing for their evening meeting. The rabbi could tell they were a little more interested than normal when they noticed the rabbi with Ann.

The rabbi, not liking to avoid situations, addressed some of the women in a happy tone, "So, you heard about our car mishap in the mountains. I'll never plan a staff meeting away from the temple again."

The women laughed appreciatively and the rabbi opened the refrigerator, saying aloud, "Ann, I still need to discuss some issues with you before I go home for dinner. I hope you don't mind joining me for a little dessert. Perhaps you'll get some paper to take down notes and I'll get the cake."

A few minutes later they were both back in the rabbi's study. The rabbi made sure the door was open and turning to Ann said, "Sorry for no wine, and there was no cheesecake. I hope the chocolate cake will work. I'm not sure if it was meant for the Hadassah meeting or was left from some other event."

"No problem. I do fine with cake, with or without wine. I do see that those rumors about us do bother you. I'm flattered. Now, what happened when you saw White Eagle? You seem in a better mood when you returned from the visit."

"I went down there thinking he was certainly guilty and I was angry that he betrayed all those who had trusted in him."

"Like yourself?" Ann injected.

Rabbi Daniels showed his exasperation. "Can you just let me talk without trying to psychoanalyze everything I say? Now, where was I...? Oh yes, the evidence was compelling and even his attorney thought there was no hope. Remember the public defender's defeated comments? Although, I have held on to the Jewish legal tradition there must be two witnesses who see the actual murder for a conviction.

"However, all the circumstantial evidence pointed to White Eagle. The physical evidence was quite strong; the fingerprints, his gun, and his being angry at her. And one doesn't usually confess, especially twice, unless they're speaking the truth. I still didn't want to believe he killed his wife," the rabbi said as he spread out his hands. "All the evidence was circumstantial except for his confessions. That was a problem for me. Under Jewish law he could not be convicted."

"What does that mean?" blurted out Ann.

"I know, you never learned about Jewish tradition growing up. Well, actually, very few Jews know about Jewish criminal law, which is really a shame. And to be honest, most rabbis don't know much about this stuff either. It's very interesting and actually contains concepts that we should be taking very seriously. Jewish law has many procedures to protect defendants, especially in a case that could involve the death penalty. The rabbis were afraid of circumstantial evidence because it could lead to convicting an innocent man. And, they didn't trust confessions. In effect, its protections about self-incrimination are much stronger than the constitution's Fifth Amendment guarantees. Hence, you had to have at least two eye witnesses, and a defendant could never testify against himself."

"Are there other differences between Jewish law and our legal system?"

"Definitely. A verdict of guilty couldn't be rendered until the next day. The rabbis wanted those making the decision to sleep on their verdict. Yet in our legal system a decision to acquit could be made the same day. A witness had to have a good reputation in the community. And, one of my favorite differences is what was told to the witnesses.

"The *Mishnah Torah*, a legal code written by the Rambam, whom I mentioned before, states, 'If one has given false testimony and it has become known through witnesses that he has testified falsely...it is a Biblical command to do to him as he intended to do to the person against whom he testified.'"

Ann sounded impressed. "Wow, you're saying that a lying witness on a capital case would be put to death. It certainly beats what we do today that doesn't seem to stop hardly anyone from lying."

Rabbi Daniels continued, "Those making the decision had to be sophisticated and know, among other things, mathematics, astronomy, medicine, and the methods of magicians." He paused and a smile crossed his face. "I guess they had to know about lawyers who are like magicians in that they can change black to white and hide things behind smoke and mirrors."

Ann laughed and the rabbi joined her. "So, what you're saying is that the Jewish tradition wanted those who decided peoples' fate to be very knowledgeable. That's a very different concept than we have. While I do like that idea, especially with the increasing use of complex evidence such as DNA, I worry it would exclude good people and create an elitist mentality. While I'm intrigued and would like to know more, I'm still bothered by the first thing you shared about the need for eyewitnesses. Are you telling me that Jewish law would allow a murderer to go free because he was smart enough to make sure that no one saw him?"

"In a way, yes. A court could not convict merely on circumstantial evidence. But remember, Ann, this reality of existence on earth is only one of the levels of reality. For the mystics, there are actually four worlds that exist simultaneously-the worlds of action, being, creation and emanation. For our rabbis, there is therefore ample opportunity for divine punishment to take place on this level at another time or on the other levels. Perhaps, when G-d shows us our life and what we could have been, that may be the greatest punishment of all."

"You know, Rabbi, I agree with you. At the same time, I think that it might give little comfort to a victim's family who is certain that a murderer might not be punished in a physical manner. I'm not sure I can blame a father for wanting to kill someone who he believes raped and killed his daughter."

Rabbi Daniels clasped his hands, saying, "I'm not sure I can blame that parent either. That person's pain is deep, his loss so unbearable and the outrage so limitless; I understand how he could want to murder. Yet, I blame a society that allows this "so-called justice" in the name of revenge. The revenge cycle was part of our human history that our Biblical ancestors attempted to stop. They created six cities of refuge where a person who accidentally killed someone could seek refuge from angry family members. Prior to that time, it was the bloody custom to avenge the death of a relative and create a cycle of killing that often took multiple lives. A society that sanctions revenge also sanctions its descent into lawlessness."

"Can I ask you a deeply personal question? I would understand if 99 you didn't want to answer." Ann's voice was very soft and her eyes had locked onto the rabbi's. Rabbi Daniels slowly nodded as if he knew what was coming.

"The man who caused the accident that took Leah's life, I never asked. What happened to him? I heard he was sent to jail for six months."

The rabbi closed his eyes as if to shut out the painful memory. "The man, his name is Matt, was convicted of reckless driving and leaving the scene of an accident."

"He left!" Ann's shocked voice reverberated in the Rabbi's office.

Slowly, Rabbi Daniels continued. "Yes. His attorney claimed he didn't realize that he had run Leah's car off the road when he quickly swerved into the right lane to get off at an approaching exit. The jury didn't believe this and he was sentenced to some jail time," the rabbi concluded in a monotone.

"You don't think he got enough, do you?" Ann's question was more like a statement.

"To save having to go one more exit because he was in a rush, he caused my wife to die. He was in jail for only six months and still today he has never apologized. I know his attorney has advised him to say nothing to me, but he is also a human being who took a life. I don't understand people like this. I know he didn't want to hurt anyone. I know that his act was not intentional. And I know everyone does reckless things sometimes in their lives. I've made quick lane changes that could have caused an accident. Usually, nothing happens more than some other driver yelling angry words or blasting their horn. And I do understand how he could have panicked and just wanted to get away. All this I know. Yet, I can't fully forgive because I'm in too much pain. And yet, I'm a rabbi who supposedly teaches forgiveness and understanding."

"Don't you think you're being a little hard on yourself?" At that moment Ann wanted to rush over and envelop him in her arms, but knew it was the wrong thing to do.

"I wanted him dead and wanted to hate him. But, when I went to court to testify about Leah, I didn't see an evil person. I saw another human being who was terrified. I didn't want to impose more suffering on him. I just wanted him to help relieve part of my anguish by taking responsibility."

"If he can't call you, have you considered calling him?"

Ann was startled with the sudden and drastic change in the rabbi's demeanor. "I should call him?" The rabbi's voice began rising, "Excuse me, but he is the one who needs to do the calling. You're asking too much. I'm not his rabbi. I am the husband of the woman he killed. The woman I loved."

"A wise man once said, 'When you put someone in jail, you become the jailer and must remain in the prison as well.'"

Rabbi Daniels smirked, "You got that from my rabbi's column in last month's temple bulletin. It's not fair to attack me with my own words. How about we drop this subject for now and just agree that sometimes humans lack humanity and that life and even justice may not always be fair."

"OK. Do you still want to tell me what happened when you went to see White Eagle?"

White Eagle was being held at the county jail pending his preliminary hearing. Rabbi Daniels went to visit him on a Sunday morning. He had never been to a jail before and he didn't know what to expect. He arrived around ten and the large parking lot was jammed. People were everywhere. On the spacious lawn area, there was a multitude of blue, red, white and checkerboard blankets as people picnicked. The rabbi parked and walked towards the massive wooden doors that spoke in their silence of strength. People were talking and laughing. Kids were playing all over the place.

Behind the foreboding doors, the mood changed. People spoke in whispers as if in church. His mind played with this theme. He saw the guards behind the plastic bulletproof windows as the untouchable priests. The inmates, who were somewhere in the bowels of this mammoth structure, were the sacrifices. And the people outside, the family and friends, were the congregants.

There were several plastic windows lined up in a row. An attendant occupied one. The rabbi walked up and the officer did not seem to notice him. "Excuse me, I'm Rabbi Daniels, and I'm here to see an inmate."

The officer didn't look up, "Visiting hours start at 10:30. Come back at 10:20 to arrange a visit."

Rabbi Daniels was not put off. He decided to use his status as clergy to bend the rules.

"Are clergy able to visit at other times?"

The officer, a tall lean man with graying hair and a dark gray uniform, took a clipboard off the wall. "Daniels, I don't see Daniels on the clergy list. I've been around here for years." Shaking his head, he said, "Sorry Rabbi. I can't let you unless you're on the list."

A booming voice broke the calm. "Hello, Rabbi Daniels. What brings you to my humble work station?"

The rabbi couldn't place the voice or the face.

A short man, rather plump and balding with brown hair, came to his rescue. "Remember me? I'm Tom Singer. My boy Bill is in Zac's class. We've met at several school functions. We had a discussion about the death penalty. I couldn't understand why some rabbis were for it and some against. I thought that Jews have an official stance."

"Mr. Singer, there is an old joke that at the parting of the Red Sea, the real miracle was not that the sea parted and the Jews were rescued. The real miracle was that for a brief time, all the Jews went in the same direction. We love to argue."

Sergeant Singer laughed. He told the officer to add the rabbi to the clergy list and let him in. The rabbi told the officer he wanted to visit White Eagle.

The first officer spoke stiffly, "We'll find your friend. Please wait here. We'll call you." He pointed to a row of metal chairs attached to the floor with metal clips. "Have a seat."

A quarter of an hour later, at exactly 10:30, hordes of people, like locusts, descended and formed ungainly lines in front of the Plexiglas windows, now flanked by an array of officers. There were people of various races, nationalities, and economic stations. To his surprise, these friends and relatives of the incarcerated seemed almost emotionless. He didn't sense any anger, fear, guilt or embarrassment; only occasional sadness from some of the older women, perhaps a mother or a grandmother, rubbing away a tear. He couldn't imagine what it was like to visit a family member in jail. At this point he didn't understand how hard it would be to see someone you care about trapped in this place.

The officer he originally spoke to waved at the rabbi from behind the Plexiglas window. He moved to the front of a long line of people, and put his head close to a small metal framed speaking hole. "Please give me your driver's license and sign the register," the officer instructed. He shoved a yellow pad through a slot in bottom of the window. Rabbi Daniels complied with his requests, and was then sent down a series of hallways-sterile hallways absent of art, color, or beauty.

He passed blank-walled administrative offices. At the end of the hall was a metal door with no handles. It was eerie. He thought he was lost and had taken a wrong turn. And, why were the halls empty? Suddenly, as if a voice was coming from heaven, he heard, "Rabbi, please stand back." The door rolled into the wall with a metallic thud. He looked up and saw the camera glaring at him. As he walked in, the door slammed behind him. The disembodied voice continued, "Please walk straight ahead." He did. This hall was also free of adornments and doors. It was a great cavern. He had a frightening thought that lay in the pit of his stomach-maybe he would be trapped in here forever.

He finally came to another metal door. Again the Wizard of Oz voice spoke, "Rabbi, please again stand back." The door slid aside. This next hall way was brightly lit. There were rows of doors on the left side with large red numbers painted on their exteriors. "Please go into room number 3. When you have finished, I'll let you out." He didn't know if the body that went with the voice could hear him, but he replied "thank you" to the camera pointed at him from the ceiling. He jumped a little when he heard, "You're welcome."

The metal door to room number 3 was heavy and hard to pull open. The room was actually two smaller rooms connected by a Plexiglas partition. The window was broken only by a metal circle with little metal bars for speaking and listening. There was a small wooden chair on each side of the window. He sat. A deep sense of depression descended upon the rabbi. The walls were a melancholy shade of dirty yellow. The rabbi's polished black shoes seemed out of place on the dingy concrete floor. A singular light bulb glowed overhead. His mind became a flood of words-desolate, forsaken, dismal, defeated, forgotten, and afraid. He didn't know what to say, what words of comfort he could offer.

The door on the other side opened and a crumpled man shuffled in with his head bowed. He was like a caged animal let in to be put on public display. This man, gray hair in disarray, was dressed from neck down in a faded red jump suit. This man no longer looked like Grandfather White Eagle. The rabbi was reminded of the time when he had seen a strong oak tree that had been hit by lightening. A fire had burned out its insides. Stripped of his regalia, his glow was all but gone. White Eagle was like that once proud oak tree.

White Eagle sat down heavily and raised his gaze in a tired fashion to meet the rabbi's. His eyes were dark and deep and showed little emotion. If he was surprised at seeing the rabbi, it didn't show. He looked like someone from another world that was both dead and alive at the same moment. The rabbi shivered.

The rabbi didn't say anything. In the Jewish tradition, when someone is mourning and you come to give comfort, you wait for him or her to speak first. The rabbi waited. The sound of a moth flying around the light bulb broke the silence.

After a few moments, White Eagle looked up. "Hello Rabbi. Thanks for coming."

The rabbi felt awkward. "How is the food?"

White Eagle chuckled, and said, "Pasta, pizza, bread, more pasta; not bad if you like starch." They sat in silence for a while. But now it wasn't as uncomfortable. The rabbi realized his mere presence was like a soft breeze in the stifling and limited routine of jail life.

When White Eagle broke the silence next, his whole body began to shake. "I can't believe that I killed Ruth." White Eagle's body continued to quiver. "I loved her so much and I miss her terribly. Rabbi, can you explain to me why I would have killed her?"

He looked at White Eagle. White Eagle was waiting for the rabbi to speak, but he didn't know what to say.

White Eagle continued, "Do you have any words of comfort for a man who kills?" His tone was of dark bitterness and remorseful self-pity. "According to your tradition, I am dammed eternally."

"White Eagle, I don't believe in hell after death. Only here on earth."

Ann interjected at this point in the story, stopping her fork in mid-air dangling a piece of chocolate cake. "Hold on. Before you tell me that I'm an ignorant Jew, a lot of people, a lot of Jewish people, don't get the idea of no hell. To be perfectly frank, I've heard you say this many times and I don't get it. Shouldn't bad people suffer for what they did?"

The subject of hell made Rabbi Daniels uncomfortable. He got up from his desk and began pacing. "Our tradition is often like a political convention with many voices debating. Some do speak of a type of hell. Most of the rabbis have no concept of hell or damnation in the way you may think. When we die, we need to come to view and deeply understand the choices we made. Rather than being punished, this process is one of learning and growing. Eventually, all souls become united with the Creator of all."

"So are you saying that a murderer like White Eagle, if he was put to death, would not be damned?"

"Ann, again let me caution you. As far as this concept of eternal hell, imagine you have a son that you love very much. And this son murdered someone in cold blood. Is that son still your son? Would you totally disown him? Would you want him to suffer extreme pain?"

The rabbi looked at Ann expectantly. Finally Ann's shoulders relaxed. "No, I would still love my son."

"That's my view of G-d, our eternal parent. G-d may want us to act a certain way and is disappointed when we don't. However, a loving G-d would never abandon us to a place of eternal darkness and pain. If there is any hell, it is only when we are too blind to feel G-d's love. And that hell is only due to our perception of being abandoned."

"So you're saying Jews feel G-d is always with us?" asked Ann.

"Yes," he replied.

"Here you go again. Taking events or thoughts and relating them to something Jewish. Do you always do this?"

"I've thought about this too. I do see life and feel the rhythm of time through Jewish lenses. Our tradition teaches us to live in this world and to use our Jewish values and teachings to help bridge what is and what ought to be. It is not always easy, but life is meant to make us choose to affirm a meaningful life."

The rabbi could tell that Ann was about to ask another question. He liked discussing philosophy, but not now. "Hold on to your other questions because what happened at the jail gets really interesting. And, your piece of chocolate cake is about to fall."

Ann realized that the chocolate cake wasn't quite sure if it was going to remain on the fork or escape. Ann took a quick vicious bite, resolving all doubt.

"By the way," the rabbi asked, "what was your next simple question?"

"Could you please explain to me the meaning of life?" They both laughed.

The rabbi told White Eagle, "I don't know your tradition, but for me hell is when I become too afraid to say the truth to myself and to the Great Spirit. Hell is only a perception that the Source of creation no longer wants or values each of us. But in truth we are each wanted and have infinite value because we are a part of the infinite One who made us."

White Eagle thought about that for a minute, "Yes, the Great Spirit is always with us, even when we get drunk and don't know what we are doing."

He then looked at the rabbi and the rabbi saw the eyes of an angry stranger or trapped animal. "Why did you come? Did you want to see what a drunken Indian looks like? Perhaps you wanted to feel good about yourself so you can go back and tell everyone what a good person you are!"

The rabbi understood his outrage and didn't take his outburst seriously. But, why was he there? "Brother, I must tell you I'm not really sure why I have come. Carol thought I could help you from a legal point of view. Frankly, I'm not sure I want to be involved. I guess I came to see a friend."

"Sorry. I'm just furious and alone. It is like being in a dream and waking up to a nightmare." He stood up, but could only take one step to each side. "I know you're a good lawyer, but my case is open and shut. I got filthy drunk after staying off the stuff for years. I woke up to find Ruth dead at my feet. My public defender, a nice enough guy, doesn't have too much hope for this old drunken fool who thought he was an elder."

It was at this point that something began to bother the rabbi. He couldn't put his finger on it, but his subconscious had just picked up something on its radar. "White Eagle, could you repeat what you just told me?"

"What, about being a fool?"

"No, there was something else. Wait!" He extended his hands to will them not to shake. "Did you say you woke up from being drunk to find Ruth dead? Does that mean that you don't remember killing her?"

The rabbi eyed him expectantly.

"Rabbi, I don't remember a thing."

He faced White Eagle. "Why did you tell the 911 operator and the police that you did it?" asked the rabbi quietly.

"She was dead, at my feet. The gun was lying next to my hand. I saw all of my sacred objects on the floor where I must have thrown them when I went to get my gun!" his voice was rising as he stood.

"Grandfather, sit down. Maybe you did kill Ruth. All the physical evidence suggests you did. Nevertheless, I'm bothered by a few things. Let me ask you a question that I want you to carefully think about before you answer. Put all the evidence aside." The rabbi put his hand on his heart, "Does this say that you killed Ruth?"

White Eagle sat down heavily and looked at his feet considering. "I have dreamed of Ruth coming to me. She is dressed in the same pure white cotton dress she wore when we got married. She extends her hands to me in love. She tries to speak but no words come out. There is no anger towards me, only love." White Eagle then raised his hand in a measured fashion to his heart and as if in a trance quietly uttered, "I don't know."

Ann interrupted again and asked, "Rabbi, did you take his dream seriously? I know there are a lot of books on dream interpretations. I'm curious, what does Judaism think of dreams?"

"At this rate, we're going to be at it again all night. And dreams are very complex things, just ask Freud and Jung. Dreams are a major part of our Biblical tradition. Virtually every major Biblical hero is influenced by dreams; Jacob and his dream of the ladder to heaven and then the dreamer of all dreamers, Joseph. However, there is not much that most rabbis do with dreams in modern times. I interpret dreams differently. Certainly dreams are a way for our unconscious to talk with us in a safer way. Dreams are a combination of our deeper reservoir of knowing and a deep spiritual communication from G-d. I take dreams as precarious communications, often from G-d, and so does our tradition. Our tradition believes that a dream that is not analyzed is like a letter never opened."

Ann smiled and said, "Now I'm snooping. Have you had any recent dreams?"

Rabbi Daniels adjusted his position on the chair, now clearly uncomfortable. "Yes, I dreamt I could not find the way to the temple. I was angry that I was going to be late. My passenger was the previous rabbi at the temple, Brad Seigle. He looked over at me in my dream and stated, 'It's okay we'll be late; as a matter of fact it's okay if we don't get there at all.'"

"Interesting dream, Rabbi."

Rabbi Daniels nodded his head.

"So, you took White Eagle's dream seriously." Ann concluded. "And I promise not to interrupt again."

For the first time, there was a glimmer of light and the rabbi wanted to fan that spark so he began to ask questions.

"White Eagle, was there anyone else who might want to have killed Ruth?"

"I don't know. I don't think so. Everyone loved her. I know that some were unhappy she wasn't a Native American. But, no, no one I know would want to hurt her."

"Who else knew that your gun was on the top shelf?"

"Only Ruth."

"Why did Ruth go to work at the casino?"

He acknowledged he didn't know. He presumed that she felt they needed more money. She was always furious when people would come for a ceremony or ask him to speak and never give him any money. She would scream at him, "How do they think we live, we can't buy food using people's appreciation. We need money to buy food."

The rabbi also noticed there seemed little antagonism in his voice when he mentioned Ruth. Rather, there was a longing. That spark of hope was getting a little brighter.

White Eagle continued to describe Ruth and how, in spite of her very ranting at all the freeloaders, she was very proud he was the tribe's elder. She would never turn anyone away and often spent time talking with women about their moon times, problems with their husbands, or their children.

White Eagle shared something that really got the rabbi's attention. He mentioned that Ruth told him right before she went to work at the casino that he had to trust her. And, she reminded him she would never embarrass him, even when she might be upset with him. This last comment made Rabbi Daniels very curious.

The rabbi took a bold step, perhaps that gambling instinct again, and told White Eagle he might be willing to be involved with his case, if it were fine with him. White Eagle agreed and even seemed somewhat relieved. The rabbi then asked him if it would be all right if he went to visit White Eagle's trailer.

White Eagle gave the Jewish leader a long sideways glance and then asked, "Why do you want to go to the house? It is now an impure place because of the murder."

"I can't say that I know the answer. I guess I have a feeling, an intuition," answered Rabbi Daniels.

White Eagle smiled for the first time. "I trust people's intuition. However, it is dangerous to visit a place where there has been death. Spirits of the dead are there. If you must go in, be sure to sage off first. And then, after you leave, sage off again."

Here was the elder speaking; it felt good to the rabbi to feel the strength of this elder come alive as once again he was taking the role of teacher. He paused and Rabbi Daniels could see he was in deep concentration. "You might need stronger medicine. The police took my small medicine bag that I usually keep tied around my neck. Perhaps, they'll allow you to bring my medicine bundle. I don't recall if it had fallen to the floor with the other ritual objects. Look for a pouch made of deerskin. If it is not on the floor, then it is still on the top shelf. Please bring it to me and treat it with respect. There is powerful sacred medicine inside. Come back and see me right after. Your life may be in danger and I may need to do a healing ceremony for you."

Ann looked at the rabbi who was now silent. "Do you really believe all this stuff that White Eagle was saying about dangerous spirits, the need for spiritual protection?"

"I do, yes. We Jewish people have believed in dangerous spirits and amulets for a long time."

"Really! Give me an example," challenged Ann.

"When we had our first children, a family friend gave us ribbon to put around the crib to keep Lilith away, one of my favorite characters in the Jewish tradition."

"To keep away who?"

"Ann, I have a lot of work to do."

"Don't you dare! Who is Lilith? I don't know my Bible well, but I'd be willing to bet there is no person by the name of Lilith. Am I right?"

"Lilith was the first woman according to our rabbinic tradition, and you are right, she is not found in the Bible. She is generally viewed by the tradition as an evil demon. She sneaks into the rooms of new children and turns their hearts against their parents. Hence the need for amulets to protect newborn babies."

"What makes her do this?"

"The tradition says she was exiled from the Garden of Eden to make room for the new woman, Eve." The rabbi, with a twinkle in his eyes, looked at Ann. "You see, during their intimate moments, Lilith wanted to be on top. Adam became angry and asked G-d for a more submissive helpmate. Hence, Eve. Lilith, however, was banished and became eternally livid."

"That's not fair!" Ann blurted out. "You mean to tell me those rabbis couldn't stand having a strong woman around the garden."

Rabbi Daniels laughed long and loud, "Ann, I told you that I like Lilith. And so do many others. There is even a Jewish woman's magazine with that title. Rabbis are beginning to write new stories to revisit this tradition in a much more positive way. So, her reputation is improving with time."

"Well, I may need to put some ribbons around my office to protect me from aggressive rabbis who tempt me with wine and cake." With that she stood up and went back to her outer office.

Chapter 7
The House

Shall we receive good at G-d's hand, and not evil?
Job

Rabbi Daniels, in a gray suit with a yellow and gray polka-dot tie and a gray leather *kippah* atop his head, walked down the concrete path leading to the temple from the front parking lot. He passed by a large black marble memorial stone where he always stopped. It listed the concentration camps in which members of his community had lost family during the Holocaust. The sense of dread, rage, and unanswered questions were ever-present chains that tied him to this past. However, around this memorial with its carved names of the camps were plants with plaques dedicated to non-Jews who risked their lives to save Jews. In addition to several individual names, the name of the country of Denmark was also honored. Its leaders and people were particularly courageous and unified in their protection of the Jewish Community. In spite of all the darkness there is always light, and maybe he would find some light for White Eagle.

He walked into the synagogue and saw Ann. There was no one else around and he confided, "Ann, I had a dream last night. One of those dreams that is as clear as real life.

"I was carrying those stones we saw at the old house when your car broke down. I can't get them out of my head. In the dream, I knew these stones were sacred. They are from a consecrated Indian site. A burial ground. All I remember is carrying the stones. What do you think it means?"

"Excuse me," she replied, "but I thought you were the rabbi. Did you tell anyone else your dream?"

"Yes, I have a friend Richard who is a psychiatrist. He joked that it meant I need more exercise. Actually, he thinks it means I'm getting in touch with part of White Eagle's past. This is getting strange but it is also getting interesting. What if this journey to help White Eagle is more about me returning?"

"I don't get your meaning?"

"The stones! Maybe they represent my spiritual path as well."

"Perhaps you're reading into all of this a little too much," Ann asked with more anxiety in her voice than she intended.

"Oh don't worry. But, I am more curious now to visit White Eagle's trailer and see what awaits me there."

"So," Ann asked in a low voice as if she were a conspirator, "when are you off to visit the murder scene?"

"Tomorrow afternoon. I thought it would be easy. But, when I called the public defender, he didn't want to help me do anything unless I told him my defense theory. He also didn't want me to play amateur detective. 'This is not like the movies where the neophyte is going to find something overlooked by the clumsy and stupid professionals,' he said to me. He finally agreed to call the assistant district attorney, who did give permission for me to visit the crime scene. I had to promise not to take anything and to guarantee that I act properly, as a detective named Markman was going to accompany me."

The rabbi had finished with his meetings and it was Tuesday afternoon. Although White Eagle often visited the preservation where Blue Star lived, White Eagle actually lived on the reservation, a much closer drive from the temple. Rabbi Daniels drove to the reservation along a mountain road. As he approached, he was aware he would have to drive through the parking lot of the casino to enter the reservation. It was the first time he realized the reservation bordered the highway by a narrow strip that now resembled a large football field. At one end was the large squat brown casino with a small neon sign announcing its presence. At the other end sat a series of connecting buildings with large glass and wooden walls housing the tribal council, and in the middle a parking lot to serve both facilities. Huge buses were disgorging swarms of brightly dressed seniors, many with cameras, excitedly allowing themselves to be swallowed up by the cavernous mouth of the casino.

There were no street signs once he was on the reservation itself. People navigated by landmarks and he followed the map he made when he was meeting with White Eagle: make a right turn at the house with the red trim, turn left when you see the white house with an old brown Jeep on bricks lying prostrate on the front lawn, look for an overgrown vacant lot and next door is a large pea green mobile trailer with white trim that needs painting. The rabbi found the trailer without getting lost. It was actually easier than he thought because there was a yellow police ribbon tied around it like a birthday present. The yard stood out like a brightly colored red rose in a thicket of weeds. In most of the other yards the grass had lost the battle for supremacy against the dirt and the weeds, but White Eagle's was as well kept as a suburban home, even though it was a trailer. Red, yellow, and white flowers bordered a surprisingly green lawn. Standing atop the verandah covered with the bright green of artificial turf was Detective Markman.

The rabbi pulled behind the detective's plain white Chevy four-door sedan. It was an undercover car with cheap hubcaps, and that special plain appearance that screams "police." The rabbi stepped over the yellow crime tape. "I'm Rabbi Daniels," he said.

The detective was as least six foot if not taller, a bald man in his late fifties, and had the body of a former football player. His strong handshake was painful. He wore a white shirt and a solid blue tie. As if the rabbi had already forgotten, Detective Markman reminded him to touch nothing. The rabbi, in mock submission, raised his right hand and vowed, "I promise to be a good tourist and not handle anything without asking permission."

The detective quickly assumed the role of tour guide, "I presume this is your first visit to an actual crime scene." The front door screen was pulled open. The detective used a key from a black folder to get in. The silver aluminum door gave way and they went into the kitchen. Besides glasses in the sink, nothing else seemed out of place. The brown tile counter surfaces were spotless and the bright blue dish towels neatly stacked. Through the kitchen was the living room, the location of the murder. On the floor was a chalk outline of how the body was found when the police came. Indeed, as if a child had drawn a sprawled body, there was the outline giving mute testimony that someone's life had ended here. Detective Markman's voice seemed inappropriately loud. Obviously to him it wasn't a sacred shrine. He continued the tour, "Those brown spots around the chalk marks are dried blood."

Rabbi Daniels had a mixture of conflicting feelings from dismay to outrage and reverence to trepidation. In the Jewish tradition, touching a dead body or being in a place where someone has died makes you ritually impure. It was a reminder that while death is inevitable; our task is to be with the living, to live in this reality.

Detective Markman continued, "The chalk circle next to the rocking chair is where the gun was found." From the black folder he pulled out some photos, "Here are the pictures of the gun on the floor. It's a rather cheap semi-automatic that can be purchased easily. It's a 25-caliber gun called a 'raven arms.' Probably costs less than a hundred bucks." The rabbi handed the pictures back to the detective.

The rabbi then saw five small circles, like five white pennies, drawn on the tightly piled beige carpet, forming a line between the gun and the chalk outline of where Ruth fell. "What are those?" asked Rabbi Daniels, pointing to the small chalk marks.

"The gun shells create a pattern. In this case, it tells us the gun was fired from the chair moving towards the victim." He pointed to the wall opposite the rocking chair. "See those four chalk circles going across the wall? Those mark bullet holes that missed. There is a fifth shot that missed," and Detective Markman pointed to a circle drawn around a hole over the door frame leading to the kitchen.

"Our theory was that in a rage, White Eagle got his gun from the top of that bookshelf over there and sat down in the rocking chair to wait for Ruth. When she came home and stood in front of him, he started firing and moved towards her. Most of the shots missed but, unfortunately, one found its mark."

"Do you think he was aiming or just firing at random?" the rabbi asked.

The detective looked at the rabbi very carefully before speaking, "The one who knows for sure will never speak. A smart defense attorney could argue he was in a drunken rage and didn't fully realize what he was doing. Rabbi, I was one of the people who came early that morning to arrest White Eagle. I was the one who tied a plastic bag on his right hand to make sure if there was any gunpowder residue it would shake off into the bag. Yes, Rabbi, there was gunpowder residue. I liked your friend. I take my kids to the annual summer parade in St. Luke's. I would point out White Eagle, this proud man as he walked in the parade representing his people. He even spoke at my kids' school and I recall how they ran home to tell me what he taught them. It's a shame he did this. He was a fine example and now he is just one more bad Indian."

The rabbi's stomach churned at this last comment. Normally, he didn't let racist comments pass. He thought of the Biblical command not to stand idly by the blood of a neighbor, which the rabbis expanded to include hateful speech. He had on occasion told people who had engaged in racial jokes that he did not appreciate their comments and found them to be offensive. He knew that there were some who felt he was too sensitive about this topic but he felt that racial jokes had been used to create dangerous stereotypes that hurt people, especially his people. He remembered how he felt when a classmate in elementary school began telling jokes about Jews being stingy. He had felt shamed and lonely when his fellow classmates only laughed at the jokes and did not sense his pain. He vowed then, although he was very young, not to let that happen to others. And he had generally kept that vow. But, he felt he had to remain quiet and so he settled into an uncomfortable silence. Getting irritated would not help White Eagle, and the rabbi felt he needed all the information he could get.

The rabbi took a breath and changed the subject, "If your theory is right, how did the gun end up next to the rocking chair?"

Detective Markman quickly replied, "After White Eagle realized what he had done, he returned to his rocking chair and sat down where the gun slipped from his hand to the floor. White Eagle admits that he remembers waking up in the rocking chair and seeing Ruth lying on the floor. He went to her and called 911 when he realized that something was wrong. And remember, Rabbi," the detective emphasized, "he confirmed in that phone call he had killed his wife. We have the tape of that call."

The rabbi ignored the detective's last comment and asked, "If there are five bullet casings and five missed shots, what about the casing for the bullet that must have killed Ruth?"

"Detective Markman pointed to another penny-size mark between where Ruth fell and a bookcase on the far wall. "That's the extra shell casing.

We think that White Eagle or the paramedics must have kicked it over there in all the excitement."

As the rabbi gazed towards the lone small chalk mark, he noticed a jumble of seemingly unrelated items that were strewn at the base of the pine pre-fab bookcase as if by a child at play. There was a long white pipe next to a drum made of a piece of stretched deerskin covering a wooden round frame. An empty brown cardboard shoebox lay on its side with a blackened white towel protruding like a tongue. The sidepiece from some broken glasses. A large eagle feather next to the box was grotesquely bent in half like a broken doll. The detective and the rabbi walked closer to the objects for a better look. "The shoe box contained the gun which was wrapped in that towel," he pointed out. "We think that when White Eagle went to get the gun, these items were pushed aside and fell to the ground. The pipe got a little chipped and that feather probably got bent from the fall."

The rabbi didn't see the medicine bundle on the floor. He told the detective that he was asked by White Eagle to find his medicine bag and take it back to him in jail if that was all right with the detective. He described the medicine bag to Markman, saying "It's a deer skin cloth wrapped around several objects and tied with a leather strap approximately twelve inches in length. White Eagle said it was with his other ritual objects that fell to the floor."

The detective checked the list of evidence taken into custody at the crime scene. There was no listing of the medicine bundle. Thinking that maybe it had not been knocked down, they checked the top shelf. Then the detective noticed the bag in-between some books on Native American culture on the middle shelf. He quickly looked inside and held up a rattle. He shook it like a toy. The rabbi cringed. He knew it was an important ritual object. The detective opened a bag and smelled the substance inside and announced in a surprised tone, "Tobacco." And then suspiciously, "What is this?" He pulled out a grayish bundle.

Rabbi Daniels remembered the sweat lodge when he first smelled the burning plant. "It's white sage used for ceremonial purposes. It's not an illegal substance." Markman let him take the medicine bag after he had the rabbi sign a receipt.

As the rabbi walked out of the house with the medicine bundle, he remembered the sage. He had forgotten to sage off before he entered the house. He drove a short distance and got out of the car at an abandoned lot and under a sparse oak tree, lit the sage, and passed it around his body as a protective cover. He hoped no one saw him, especially a congregant, as he felt a little silly. He recalled watching Blue Star light the sage and then blow out the fire. He did the same and thought about Jewish beliefs around purity and impurity. After a funeral, Jews wash their hands when leaving the cemetery or upon entering a house of mourning. The washing doesn't involve soap, because this is a spiritual, not a physical cleansing. He remembered to lift his feet, right and then left, as he continued to encircle his body with the smoke of the sage. He was no longer self-conscious; he was feeling cleansed and waved his free hand to more deeply inhale the fragrance of the sage.

Chapter 8
The Healing

Every one entrusted with a mission is an angel.
Maimonides

✷**R**abbi Daniels returned to the synagogue. His head felt stuffy, his breathing was labored, and it was hard for him to focus. Ann was walking toward him down the hallway. When she spied the rabbi her curiosity was apparent. "What was it like being at a real murder scene? Do you still think he's guilty?" When she got close enough to see the white of his face, Ann's questioning stopped abruptly. "Are you okay?"

"I'm not feeling great. I must have gotten that flu that's going around."

With a note of concern in Ann's voice, "I'm going to cancel the rest of your appointments. It's to home for you. I'll let Brenda know to expect a sick rabbi."

Rabbi Daniels had a fitful night. Brenda came in a few times asking him if he was feeling okay. His children, especially Rachael, seemed overly concerned. He rarely got sick and knew that the children were easily frightened since Leah died. He reassured them while at the same time becoming more alarmed himself as he had never felt like this before.

The rabbi's mind kept remembering the house, the chalk outline of Ruth's body, the various objects on the floor, and White Eagle's face behind the Plexiglas barrier. He didn't know how much sleep he got. He awoke with a headache that tore at his eyes. It was similar to one that had been described in an old aspirin commercial, like two male bucks were fighting right above his forehead. His mouth was dry as if he had been wandering in the desert for 40 years. His body ached all over and his head was hot to the touch. Brenda brought him tea and urged him to stay in bed. However, White Eagle's warning about going to the house continued to reverberate in his head.

Brenda brought chicken soup, Leah's special recipe, which usually cured everything from the flu to an ingrown toenail. He was so delirious that he asked for "Leah" to read to him. It was their custom that when either of them got sick, they would lie next to each other and read. This always made the rabbi feel better. When he awoke in the morning, he felt his head and knew that his temperature was up. He was sure he felt Leah next to him and heard her tell him to go to White Eagle. This surprised him as Leah would usually have barred his escape from bed when he was feeling sick. For some reason, the rabbi trusted what he thought he had heard. He told himself that if it were just his imagination, his next stop would be with their doctor or the emergency room. Brenda got the kids off to school and he slowly got his aching body dressed and drove to the jail.

119

Unlike the rabbi's first visit to the county jail, there were few cars in the parking lot and no families picnicking on the grass. The sun had been up-staged by dark clouds that matched his darkening mood. He didn't like this place of bricks and mortar that held so much hurt and fury. Since the time for normal visiting hours had long since passed, there was no one at the Plexiglas window. He stood there quite awhile, leaning on the window for support, and then began knocking on the glass to get someone's attention. This time his name was on the list and he only had to wait a few minutes until he was told by the pale looking guard that he could enter the inner belly of the jail. Soon the rabbi was sitting in the gloomy cubicle again with his thoughts, but he was having a hard time keeping his head up.

Finally, the door opened and White Eagle entered. Rabbi Daniels automatically stood up. White Eagle smiled a genuine smile. There was even a twinkle in his dark black eyes surrounded by trails of wrinkles. "Why do you stand?" he asked.

"I stand for an elder. There is a rabbinic statement that translates, 'Stand for the one with white hair.' Not the gray hair of an old person, rather, a person with wisdom, an elder. I stand, White Eagle, for you."

Although the rabbi still thought White Eagle was probably a murderer, he also thought of him as a damaged human being who was vanishing before the rabbi's eyes. The rabbi, feeling weak, wanted to help him remember who he was, a man of dignity and a man of the spirit. This act - of the rabbi standing upon his entry - helped to jog his internal memory of being an elder. White Eagle straightened up and the rabbi could actually see the beginnings of a faint glow that grew from White Eagle's body. White Eagle gradually and deliberately sat down. He looked at the rabbi for a long time, his eyes like ageless windows looking beneath his body into his inner being, "You have come at a strange hour. I was in the middle of a breakfast with powdered scrambled eggs. They don't usually allow visitors at this time. I guess you're special. Tell me, why do you look dead?"

120

Rabbi Daniels related how he had gone to the murder scene. He had forgotten to pick up sage and only smudged himself after he had left.

White Eagle, rather than being compassionate, laughed at the rabbi, "You are an ignorant White man trying to play at being an Indian." The comment hurt and seemed out of place. The rabbi, already having a hard time focusing his mind, rallied with his own question. "Why are you insulting me?"

White Eagle reacted in a strange way. His eyes turned towards the rabbi as if he was an arrow and the rabbi was the target. He aimed his words, "You are part of the majority who took our land, killed our children, our culture, and our future. You have no idea what it is like to be hunted, despised and destroyed. And now I'm locked up and you've come to me for help." He looked at Rabbi Daniels, full of rage, daring him to respond.

The rabbi raised his head in anger to match White Eagle's. "I'm told you have a saying, 'Don't judge another until you have walked in his moccasins.' We have a similar saying, 'Every person has their time.' Before you place me in a neat and tight box, maybe you should see who I am and understand the history of my people. My people too have been forced from their land and had their property taken. My people have also been on forced marches where their captors watched them die. Our parents have also seen their children die for no reason other than that they were different. I know you carry the pain of your people like a sack of heavy rocks that makes your spirit sink to the depths of mother earth. Look in my eyes and see the pain of generations and search my heart to unlock its yearning to be at peace. In many ways, we are not so different." The rabbi's face had gone beet red, barely able to contain his outrage, and he said harshly: "Don't judge me, 'brother,' until you know me!"

This outburst from the rabbi must have shocked White Eagle. "I was told that the Holocaust was exaggerated by the Jews to get sympathy. I can see in your eyes that the Holocaust was true."

The rabbi couldn't believe in this place of gloom he now had to go into his people's dark memory. How could people deny all the evidence? What was their reason? This was just too much and he wanted to get up and leave. Nevertheless, although his head was throbbing, he decided to stay. "There are a lot of deniers who alter facts and simply tell people it couldn't have happened. People often believe what they want to believe. It is easier for some to forget, and some don't want to be bothered. That's why we keep talking, teaching and hoping we don't forget so we won't ever allow another genocide to take place. Unfortunately, it continues. Still, we must rage against it, if for no other reason than to prove our humanity."

White Eagle thought for a moment, "I suppose what you say makes sense. And, it is important to remember. Perhaps you talk about it too much."

The rabbi, barely able to follow the thread of White Eagle's arguments, responded, "People are already forgetting! We want people to remember so they don't forget. Even with all the pictures, the testimonies, the concentration sites, the empty synagogues, the ravaged Jewish presence in Europe and even testimony from so many of the perpetrators detailing what they did, some believe it didn't happen."

White Eagle smiled a sad smile. "People like to forget, to say it never happened. We are similar. We have our histories and we have our memories and we have our need to teach. I'm sorry I was so hard on you. I needed to lash out and you were here at the wrong time." White Eagle paused, looking very intently at the rabbi. "I'm sorry I didn't look deeper. Your soul has been touched at the house and you need a healing. Did you find my medicine bag?"

The rabbi told him that he had it in the car. White Eagle asked him if he knew any of the guards. Rabbi Daniels told him he knew Tom Singer. White Eagle knocked on the white metal door behind him and when a guard appeared, he whispered something to him. A few moments later, Tom appeared in the door way behind White Eagle. Tom looked at the rabbi as White Eagle spoke to him. He then reached into his thick black belt, which looked like Batman's utility girdle. He produced a pair of handcuffs and placed them on

White Eagle's outstretched hands. There was a knock on the door behind the rabbi and then it opened.

A guard led him back to the entrance of the jail. He told the rabbi to get the medicine bag. It was in a plastic bag in the trunk of his car. When he returned, the guard examined the bundle. He rifled past the medicine and sage but carefully scrutinized the rattle. The guard wanted to make sure it couldn't be used as a weapon. He gave the rabbi back the bundle and led him down another hallway, through two metal doors that again opened automatically; Tom brought White Eagle in and removed his handcuffs. White Eagle sat down on one of the chairs and Tom came over to the rabbi. "The chief here says that you're very sick and he needs to heal you. You do look rather rough around the gills. I don't believe in all this stuff, but I didn't think it would hurt. I told him I would have to stay here. Is that okay?" he asked. The rabbi nodded in approval.

Tom went to the far side of the rectangle room with its white walls and nondescript gray linoleum. White Eagle dipped into the white plastic shopping bag and took out the leather bundle. He turned it reverently over in his hands, "There have been many fingers touching this."

"Yes, I apologize," revealed the rabbi. "I used some of the white sage to smudge myself after leaving your house."

White Eagle nodded, obviously not happy his pouch had been violated by so many hands. He cautiously unwrapped the bundle and removed the tobacco pouch, the remaining sage, and the rattle. He looked up at the rabbi, "Where is the eagle feather?"

The rabbi looked back with a blank look. "There was no eagle feather. There was an eagle feather on the floor in front of the bookcase. It was bent. By the way, the bundle was not on the top shelf, you must have forgotten. It was the second to the top shelf." White Eagle stared, and then nodded.

"We have much to talk about," he declared as he stood, "but now you must get better." He looked over at Tom, asking, "Is it okay if I light this sage and help cleanse this room?" The rabbi was surprised when Tom nodded approval. White Eagle took a match from a small compartment in the pouch. He lit the sage and blew it out. He blew again and the sage glowed with the infusion of his breath. He waved it around the room as he sang. Rabbi Daniel's head was so tired that he just closed his eyes and felt his whole body sag into the chair. The chanting appeared to be far away, across time and space. A while later, he heard a rattle climbing the ladder of his senses. It was loud, then soft, it was following a regular beat and then it slowed down.

The rabbi awoke on a cot, not knowing where he was. Another officer was sitting nearby. "Hello, Rabbi. You've been sleeping for several hours. Are you feeling better?" The rabbi was feeling better. The officer continued, "Tom's shift ended awhile ago and he went home. He told me to let you sleep. But he asked that I call him when you woke up."

After the rabbi used the phone in the jail infirmary to call Brenda and the kids to say he was feeling better, he then called Tom. Tom was happy to hear the rabbi's voice and that he was feeling better. He also told the rabbi he had arranged for White Eagle to keep his medicine bag, as it was a religious object, and that White Eagle wanted to see him as soon as the rabbi woke up.

When the rabbi was led back to the familiar but still unfriendly cubical, he presumed that White Eagle wanted to see how he was doing, like a doctor examining a patient to see if the surgery had been successful. This time, White Eagle was already seated and stood up when the rabbi came in.

"I stand for an elder of his people," White Eagle announced in a respectful tone.

He stared at the rabbi for a minute and finally nodded his head as he sat down. "You are looking better. Your spirit seems much stronger."

"I'm feeling much better. Thank you very much. Is there anything else I should do?"

"Perhaps take two aspirin and call me in the morning," White Eagle jested. He then asked, "You told me last night you found the medicine bundle on the second to the top shelf, is that correct?"

The rabbi nodded.

"You also told me the eagle feather was not inside but was on the floor, along with other items that fell from the top shelf."

The rabbi nodded again.

"The medicine bag is always on the top shelf and the eagle feather is always inside." White Eagle insisted.

The rabbi's mind actually went blank for a moment. "Are you sure?" he asked.

White Eagle looked directly into the rabbi's eyes and said, "Yes."

The silence that followed was finally broken by the rabbi. "When was the last time you used your medicine bag?"

Thinking for a moment before answering, White Eagle responded, "The week before. I led a man's sweat as part of a healing ritual."

Memories of attending this ceremony and staying up all night around a large fire at once flashed in the rabbi's mind. His body ached, the front part of it burned hot from the fire, his back cold and stiff in the evening, his bottom in pain from sitting on the hard ground. It was a night of sharing stories and songs until the sun peeked over the purple mountains. Everyone had stood facing east and welcomed the sun with the song. Its warmth brushed their faces.

The rabbi asked if he specifically remembered returning the bundle to the top shelf and if he was sure it contained the eagle feather.

He gradually nodded his head. For some unexplained reason, this information was comforting. This was the first time Rabbi Daniels felt a tremor run through his body as he seriously contemplated that White Eagle might not have murdered his wife. But who did and why?

"I know I asked you this before, but really think about my question before you answer. Is there anyone you know who may have wanted to murder Ruth and then blame you?"

His posture collapsed as he absorbed the impact of the rabbi's question. He shook his head from side to side. The rabbi wanted to reach through the Plexiglas to White Eagle and put his hands on this man's shoulders as he began to sob.

The rabbi asked another painful question. "Were you so drunk that someone could have come in and shot a gun without you knowing it?"

White Eagle's ancient head, crowned with white hair, started to move up and down.

"I asked you before and I am going to ask you again. Do you think you killed Ruth?" It was so silent that the rabbi could hear the rhythm of his breath. He needed to hear a confirmation from White Eagle again. Finally White Eagle sighed, "I don't know."

They again sat in silence only broken by White Eagles occasional sighs.

Rabbi Daniels next asked, "Tell me about the gun. When did you get it?"

"A long time ago, maybe ten years."

"Why?"

"I just didn't trust people."

"You mean, you didn't trust Whites, is that correct?"

"No. My wife is White," and then he added more slowly, "My wife was White. And, there are good and bad people in every group. I was worried about bad people and I'm too old to fight someone with my fists. Since I have a record of armed robbery, I couldn't get a gun legally, but I wanted to have one to protect Ruth and myself."

"Did you keep the gun loaded?"

"Yes."

"Who knew you had a gun?"

"Ruth knew and maybe a few others. I'm not really sure."

The rabbi thought about this exchange and the comment White Eagle made earlier when Ruth had told him she would never embarrass him. "I want to talk to some of Ruth's friends, especially those at the Casino."

He turned to look at the rabbi. "Why at the casino?"

"I don't really have a good reason. Perhaps it's because I still don't understand why she went to work there. I'm confused and I think that by understanding Ruth's motivation it will help to put the pieces of this puzzle together. Otherwise, I think we're lost."

Chapter 9
The Casino

A gambler always loses. He loses money, dignity and time.
Maimonides

Sue was about to knock on the rabbi's door for her regular meeting when she realized that she was not alone.

"Can I help you?" Ann asked, taking her role as guardian of the rabbi very seriously.

While pointing to her rather garish blue and gray Swatch watch, Sue explained "I have a three o'clock appointment with the rabbi."

Ann was carefully dressed with dark blue shoes that matched her pressed blue skirt. "I'm Ann Goldberg, the rabbi's secretary. We met on several occasions and I know you see him every other week. I'm sorry, but he is on an important phone call. Will you please come with me and I will let him know you are here as soon as he is finished." Without giving time for Sue to protest, Ann turned on her heels and led the way to her office down the hall. She knew it was Sue who began the process that led the rabbi eventually to White Eagle. She also knew Sue was much younger than her and hoped the rabbi didn't find Sue too intriguing.

Sue sat down across from Ann's desk. Unlike Rabbi Daniels', this desk had paper placed in neat stacks. The phone seemed to ring incessantly. It seemed everyone wanted the rabbi. Ann was an expert at maneuvering to get the caller to talk to someone else. "Mrs. Smith, the rabbi would love to talk with you. However, he will be unable to get back to you due to a recent death of one of our congregants. I am sure he would want your problem addressed immediately and therefore let me put you directly through to the director of education." It was like a game. Everyone wants to talk with the rabbi and

Ann's job was to let very few ever get to him. Sue began to realize she was one of the lucky ones who were able to see the rabbi on a regular basis. She wondered what it would be like to be unable to see everyone who wanted to see you, to be unable to meet all the needs of those who wanted your time.

It took twenty minutes before the rabbi called to ask Ann to show Sue in.

"Shalom, Sue," Rabbi Daniels said as he glanced up from his computer. "I'm sorry for the delay."

Sue replied, "You are one of the busiest people I know. It's as if you have all these monkeys on your back demanding attention."

Rabbi Daniels smiled a sad smile, "It is both a wonderful blessing and a curse." He lifted up his right palm, "On the one hand, I have over 600 families which means roughly 1,500 potential congregants who all think they have the right to talk with me when they want. Moreover, they want me to serve their needs as they expect. On the other hand," the rabbi lifted up his left palm, "it truly is an honor to be invited into people's personal lives. I really love helping people and believe I am doing holy work. It's the balance that is hard," he concluded while moving one palm up and the other palm down as if they were scales.

He lowered his hands and returned to the computer to add a few more words. He then deliberately turned his chair to face Sue. She noticed that his usually joyful disposition was gone. He looked tired. He stroked his graying beard. "I'm finishing a eulogy which I will be giving in a short time. I wanted us to get started as soon as possible because I will have to leave early for the funeral."

"Rabbi, we don't have to meet now if this is a bad time. We can meet later."

Rabbi Daniels gestured with his right hand for her to sit down across from him in one of the stylish leather chairs while he kept his left hand stroking his beard. "It's fine, I'm able to switch emotions. Since I've almost finished the eulogy, I don't feel pressured."

"How can you do that...how can you be there for yourself and for others? It's like you are playing a game in which you are losing yourself." Sue wasn't sure if this last comment was overstepping appropriate boundaries. The rabbi didn't seem to notice or care.

"Sue," the rabbi began in somewhat of a patronizing tone, "I want to be present for you to answer your questions, I need to do this funeral and then come back and write my sermon for services and after that have a meeting with a bar mitzvah family. I am required to be able to switch gears quickly. If I let my emotions take control, I won't be any good for anyone. I really am required to keep calm and keep sane so others can feel safe. But right now, I'm getting a little tired of your psychoanalytic questioning. You seem to be judging me and I don't appreciate that. If you have a question, I'll answer it."

"I think you are paying a high price for being a rabbi," Sue quipped, perhaps a little too quickly, but now she was fuming. "Alright, if you want to answer my questions, I'm not going to let you get off with an easy one. And, I am not going to back off. I want to find out how and why you became a rabbi and why you're willing to put up with all these demands?"

The rabbi was already thinking about the upcoming funeral and had become somewhat confused with Sue's comments and question. "What were we talking about?"

Her anger dissipated as she saw how exhausted he was, so she simply replied, "Well, let me make it simpler. How did you become a rabbi?"

Rabbi Daniels again looked at his wooden framed clock on the wall and then at Sue and said, "Sure, the short version. And, don't interrupt me with any more of your questions.

"I didn't become a rabbi until I was already a lawyer. And, I never wanted to be a congregational rabbi. I was searching. I wanted daily spiritual practices that would connect me more deeply to my inner-self and my tradition. I felt alone and I sensed that no amount of material success would feed the deep longing that I was feeling in my life as a lawyer. So I quit my law practice. I wasn't married then and I took my savings and entered rabbinical school at the age of 30.

"It was a five year program. The first year was spent in Israel learning Hebrew and history. The next two years were in Los Angeles immersing myself in texts and tradition. The following two years I was a student rabbi in Brooklyn. I already had inklings that becoming a congregational rabbi was like becoming a CEO-it was becoming a spiritual leader based on having a piece of paper and not necessarily because I had deep and personal experience of G-d. I didn't know ways of sharing deep spiritual experiences or how to empower and guide other people to seek their own personal experiences of G-d. But being a rabbi nowadays can be more like being an administrator of a large corporation and trying to keep all the Board members and all the employees happy all the time. Nevertheless, I felt I would be different and keep the focus on being a teacher, a counselor and a spiritual leader. In spite of the realities, I do find this more rewarding than the practice of law. But there were some great things about the practice of law, such as helping people. For example, I helped Blue Star stay on his land."

Rabbi Daniels stood up, ready to end the session and then abruptly added, "However, as rabbi's become more like CEO's, carrying everyone's burden of being the official Jew made me feel even more alone. Perhaps that's why the sweat was so powerful. I have had many personal and deeply spiritual experiences and the sweat was one of them. But right now I need to say Shalom to you and help a grieving family remember how to breathe and continue living."

As the rabbi left the synagogue and started the ten-minute drive to the cemetery, he realized he was paying more attention to his mood than normal. Perhaps the morning sessions with Sue and her questions put him in a reflective disposition. While the time issues were significant and some people could get under his skin, he realized he looked forward to meeting with converts and he loved their questions. They made him think. The more difficult the question, the more he enjoyed the encounter. There was Nick, a retired fireman. Nick loved to read; he'd bring in Buber and ask the Rabbi to explain "I and Thou concepts." Rather than give a glib answer, he re-read some Buber and retrieved his notes from rabbinic school from his old dusty faded blue binder that he had kept. He was impressed he even knew where he had stored it.

Then there was Emily, a legal secretary at a local law firm. She had always felt Jewish and could never quite believe in the divine mystery of her parent's religion. It was her parents who gave her permission to come to the synagogue and begin studying. She would bring in quotes from the "Old" Testament, which she was taught was about Jesus, for the rabbi to explain why they did not pertain to Jesus. The rabbi also enjoyed the scholarship of these sessions, as he drew out various translations and showed her how these were actually interpretations, often attempting to support a particular theological point of view. And then he would show her the phrase in the actual Hebrew.

He especially remembered when she wanted to discuss the concept that Mary was a virgin. She showed the rabbi the English Biblical quote from her Bible and asked if it actually meant that the mother of Jesus was a virgin. The rabbi refused to give her a quick answer, much to her annoyance. Rather, he pulled multiple Bibles from his bookshelf to the point that he had an armload. Emily was initially surprised the rabbi had a whole shelf of Bibles from various religious traditions. And then she noticed he had several shelves of religious books from a great variety of Western and Eastern traditions. She told the rabbi she couldn't imagine her minister having those books in his study. The rabbi opened the Bibles to the same Biblical section in each and she was amazed as they compared the similar line and saw a variety of translations from "virgin" to simply a "young girl."

Emily realized a major part of her theology growing up was based on a single word that was subject to substantial interpretation. And then the rabbi showed her the Hebrew, the original language of the Bible, and they examined each word for its possible meanings. But still he refused to tell her the "right" meaning as he had warned her she had to do more than just look at the meaning of one word. He had her look at the whole Biblical section-the sentences before and after. In this context, he asked her to tell him what she thought the word meant. And, that was still not enough. He then assigned her some books that spoke about the history of the time when that particular part of the Bible was written. After all that, he remembered how she had come back to his office, slammed a stack of books on his desk, and announced the best translations would be "young" girl because there was no way to support a definitive translation of "virgin."

Emily then told him she enjoyed this in-depth study of the "Old" Testament. The rabbi hated this term as it implied the Jewish Bible was "old" and therefore outdated. He always used the terms "Hebrew Bible" and "Christian Bible." His Christian friends disliked the term "Christian Bible" as it was seen by them as cutting their Bible in two. The rabbi always responded that they had already done that by using the terms "Old Testament" and "New Testament," and that they could just as easily say their tradition includes both the Hebrew and Christian Bibles. Or, perhaps Christians could use the term "The Jesus Scriptures" instead of New Testament and therefore the "Christian Scripture" would include the Hebrew Scriptures and the Jesus Scriptures. The rabbi knew the issue was more complex and had strong historical roots; he just wished there was more honoring of the Jewish traditions' contribution.

He was amused he had these thoughts and realized that he did enjoy being a rabbi when he was affecting personal lives. And that is why he now better understood his nervousness as he prepared to go to the funeral. He had worked hard to make the eulogy honest and insightful. This would be, for many, the first time and perhaps the last time they heard the story of this man's life. He would be creating a memory and he hoped he did it well. And although he was anxious, he would not have traded this honor for anything else. He had a personal tradition of standing by the coffin to silently ask the decedent for permission to conduct his or her funeral and prayed what he did would be sufficiently worthy.

Although the rabbi had been in his office that morning to write the eulogy and meet with Sue, he had taken the previous day off to recover from his illness and to visit the casino. When the rabbi returned from the cemetery, he knew Ann was very curious and would quiz him about his conversation with White Eagle. True to form, Ann came to his office as soon as he had a break in his schedule between the phone calls and meetings. After he reviewed the events and White Eagle's revelations about the medicine bag, Ann didn't quite understand why it was important for the rabbi to visit the casino to talk with Ruth's co-workers.

Rabbi Daniels stared out the window, "One doesn't usually do something that makes someone you love become very angry without a very good reason."

Ann replied, "But how do you know she loved White Eagle when she went to work at the casino? He had reverted to his earlier pattern of getting drunk. He wasn't bringing in money. He was feeling sorry for himself. I'm sorry, Rabbi, but if I was her, my love for him would have taken a vacation."

131

"Ann, remember Blue Star and Carol? Well, they call me whenever they go to Gus' tavern to get the latest news. They love grandfather and don't want to believe he could have killed Ruth. One thing they continually tell me is that Ruth was in love with White Eagle and wouldn't have done anything to embarrass him. If they are right, it doesn't make sense to me that she went to work at the casino."

Ann glanced up, "I suppose you'll tell me that some Talmudic reasoning led you to this conclusion."

"No. My deduction was based on the old principle that if something doesn't make sense, then it doesn't make sense."

Ann smiled. "I didn't know you've been in contact with Blue Star and Carol. How are they doing?"

"It's interesting. They've been more worried about me than White Eagle. For instance, you were here when I wouldn't share my defense theory with the public defender. I was conflicted about being involved in the first place and was not sure if my ego was getting the best of me. Blue Star helped me stay centered. He heard my concerns and helped me explore my feelings, even with his own issues of trying to pay back the loan from the casino. They are putting a lot of pressure on him, and White Eagle was trying to protect the Preservation. Blue Star told me White Eagle had even told someone at the casino to forgive the loan since the casino was making so much money. He was told to butt out unless he wanted to get hurt. Blue Star didn't think anyone would try to hurt White Eagle. I even sketched for him my defense strategy, which he didn't fully understand. When I asked him if I should share the theory with the public defender, he said, 'All that you can control is your own integrity and if it doesn't feel right, you must listen to your feelings.'"

The rabbi paused for a moment.

"Carol is something else," he declared. "She helped me understand Ruth. I asked questions that sometimes caused her pain, but she would always answer. Once I asked her why a White woman would marry a Native American and vice versa."

"Carol told me that she and Ruth were friends, and this topic had come up before. She shared, 'Native Americans, even leaders such as Blue Star and White Eagle, are very proud of their heritage and yet yearn to be accepted by

White society. Ruth and I knew we were loved and, at the same time, we understood we were a sign, a prize, that they had made it.' I recall Carol making this comment in a neutral, matter-of-fact manner with no bitterness that I could detect. She then continued, 'Why did we marry them? I can't speak for all non-Indians, but Ruth and I were very similar. We'd had difficult childhoods and did not feel that we really belonged to a family. We were looking for a family that would take us in and smother us with their traditions. And, perhaps we felt guilty about what had happened to the Indians in our country and wanted to help.'"

Rabbi Daniels had a hard time sitting in one position. He stood up. "She also told me something else. She thought maybe White Eagle had killed Ruth to kill that part of him that craved the need for the White man's acceptance. Maybe I'm still grasping at straws because I need White Eagle to be innocent to help me regain my trust in people of faith. Maybe he did do it. I'm just an amateur pretending to be a detective." He walked towards the window and looked out into the sky.

Ann asked another question. "You haven't mentioned the public defender at all. Well, perhaps it is time for you to talk with him and tell him your theory. Perhaps White Eagle will need a defense. Are you in contact with the lawyer?"

"We talk periodically. He's curious about what I saw at the house and what I've been discussing with White Eagle. He also keeps asking me about the creative defense theory I had and is upset that I won't share it with him. To be honest, I rather enjoyed not telling him. I'm not sure he really cares all that much. He confided in me he thought this was just another drunken Indian who killed his wife and that my efforts were noble, but a waste of time."

"Excuse me, but this guy seems rather racist!" She pointed her finger at the rabbi to make her point, saying, "Don't you try and defend him."

"No, I'm not going to do that. But, I really don't want to tell him my defense theory. If White Eagle did kill Ruth, I don't want to be a party to getting him off. I want him to take responsibility for his actions." Rabbi Daniels contemplated this last statement. "I wonder if I'm talking more about White Eagle or Matt."

"Who?" asked Ann.

"The man who killed my wife. I didn't like the tactic of his attorney claiming he didn't know he had run my wife off the road just so he could get a lesser sentence."

Ann was resolute, "Yes, but what if it were true and he didn't know. And, what if White Eagle was in such a state of despair he could not control his actions. Do you really want to be the judge, the jury, and the jailer?"

The rabbi sighed. "By the way, last night the synagogue president came over to see how I was doing. It was very nice of Nate. I wonder how he found out I wasn't feeling so well?" With that comment he looked at Ann who lowered her eyes. "Thanks for thinking of me," the rabbi stated. "Since he was at the house to see how I was doing, I told him I probably wasn't going to renew my contract. Then I took the kids out for hot fudge sundaes to celebrate."

"Congratulations are in order," she offered without any enthusiasm whatsoever. "Did he accept your resignation?"

"No, he asked me to take some time off first before making a final decision. You know, it was strange. When I told the kids I was thinking of leaving, they didn't react the way I thought. Yes, they told me that they wished I wasn't so busy and preoccupied. At the same time, they told me they were proud of what I was doing. And that they knew their mother was proud her husband is a rabbi."

"I always thought you had smart kids. I like the president's idea. Take some time. You're going to miss a lot. You're going to miss me. And I'm going to miss you," Ann quickly averted her eyes as she surprised herself with her last comment.

"I know. That's the real reason I went out for ice cream, to cheer me up. I need to take some time off."

"So, when are you going to start taking time away from us?" Ann inquired.

"Actually yesterday, I went to the casino."

"What? You went to drink and gamble?" Ann was incredulous.

"Wow lady. What happened to that sensitive confidante I thought was sitting in front of me, the one who would stand by my side against the mob we often call congregants? And, for your information, they do not serve liquor on the floor of the casino."

"Really? When I go to Vegas I see all those cute cocktail waitresses with their skirts up to their rear trying to get all the pigeons, I mean customers, plastered so they won't mind losing their nest eggs. Are you telling me the Indian casino wants their visitors to be careful and wise gamblers so they won't lose their money too fast?"

"You are on a roll. You seem to know a lot about Vegas. Have you gone there recently and didn't tell any of us?"

"I do have a private life you are not entitled to know about. And while we are honest with each other, we don't have to share everything. So, why don't they serve liquor at the Indian casino?"

"In Vegas, one has to be 21 to gamble, which coincidentally is the same age to drink. The Indian casinos, on Native land, allow gambling at age 18 but the drinking age is still 21. They'd rather hook them younger and feel rather confident they'll be able to take their money just as fast whether they are drunk or not. By the way, what do you play?"

"Nosey, aren't you? Craps. I like the action."

"I don't understand the game myself," confessed the rabbi. "I'm told you can win a lot though."

A sardonic smile crossed Ann's mouth, "I wouldn't know. Whatever I win I seem to lose in the end."

"Ever hear about walking away when you're ahead?"

"Ever hear of keeping your mouth shut?" Ann responded in jest. "So, why did you go to the casino if not to drink away your troubles?"

"White Eagle gave me the names of three women who worked with Ruth at the casino. He thought they might be able to give me more information about Ruth. He also suggested I talk to Morning Breeze, who is on the Indian council. Even though he was still angry that Morning Breeze had changed his vote to support the casino's construction, he still respects him and feels he is a friend."

The rabbi drove the same road he had taken earlier to visit White Eagle's trailer. He walked into the casino and was met by darkness filled with the oppressive smell of smoke. As his eyes became accustomed to the low light, he saw a sea of slot machines before him, broken up with the surging waves of people mingling. He asked a passing change attendant if she knew a Linda White Cloud. After being directed to where she worked, behind the change booth near the large web of empty tables that were usually filled for bingo, the rabbi found Linda. She was very open and willing to talk during her lunch break as soon as the rabbi told her that he was trying to help White Eagle. Her favorite place to eat was the Stone Pancake House just down the road from the casino. She preferred talking there.

Linda was five feet tall, pleasingly plump with long black hair tied in a braid and a happy-go-lucky smile. The rabbi liked her. She ordered the cholesterol special: cheese omelet, hash browns and pancakes on the side. Rabbi Daniels had to restrain his parental instincts when she doused her pancakes with blueberry syrup. He ordered a fruit salad and Lipton tea. They talked about their mutual friends, Blue Star and Carol. The rabbi hadn't fully realized until then how well everyone knew everyone else and everyone's business within the local Native American community. She was fully aware who he was and what he had done for the Owl Preservation. And she knew he was trying to help White Eagle.

A few mouthfuls of pancakes and eggs loosened her up. She had known Ruth since she married White Eagle around five years ago. She knew Ruth was both very happy and very sad, someone who loved helping people and loved White Eagle. At the same time, Ruth felt people took advantage of White Eagle's good nature. People would come over to the house at any hour and make themselves at home. It was as if White Eagle and Ruth were surrogate parents. Men sought White Eagle's advice or asked him to perform ceremonies. Often women talked with Ruth about women's things or about their husbands. Drinking, child abuse, and spousal abuse are major problems on the reservations. Ruth had a good ear, a good heart, and a wise mind. And while Ruth loved helping, the fact that people would come whenever they wanted began to wear on her patience. Moreover, they expected to be fed, even when Ruth and White Eagle had little themselves. Ruth began to tell White Eagle he had to set limits on when people could come over. She asked him to charge or at least ask people to bring food when they visited. He told her this was not the Indian way. She loved him, but she hated living in poverty. She loved the traditions which White Eagle embodied but hated the reality of the reservation.

The rabbi had heard most of this before but asked his real question, why she thought Ruth went to work at the casino. "They were simply running out of money and it was the only job in town. She felt she had no option," she said. Linda revealed that Ruth hated and felt degraded being a change "girl" at the smoke filled, tourist-infested place, but she had no choice.

The rabbi then asked her if White Eagle was angry about Ruth's decision. The answer rocked the rabbi and his newfound hope. "While I liked Ruth, she was married to an elder and knew what she was getting into. Although she was not like us, she never should have disgraced her husband in public. I don't blame him for getting drunk and doing what he did."

Ann was incredulous, "This 'Linda' actually approved of what White Eagle did? I can't stand women who perpetuate these sexist systems that have kept women down throughout history. Men were created first in the Bible, so I guess they think that gives them eternal authority to knock us down and even kill us when we get out of line."

"Ann, these interruptions are going to make this report to you even longer than it is. However, just for the record, I don't believe that Adam was created first."

"Oh, some more rabbinic stories to change the misogynist Biblical text. I've read the Bible, at least the first few chapters, and I've heard all the stories. There was Adam and then from his rib came Eve. You want to tell me that the Bible lies?"

"I'm glad to see you have an open mind on this," the Rabbi observed sarcastically. "In Genesis there are two separate stories of the creation of people. The second one is the familiar one in which, according to the translators, G-d takes a rib from a sleeping Adam to create Eve. However, the Hebrew word for 'rib' can also mean 'side.' So maybe the Biblical writers really wanted to report that G-d took a 'side' of Adam to make Eve."

Ann began to laugh. "Give me a break! I've never heard this before."

"Now, before you continue to laugh and say that I'm manipulating the text, let me tell you about the first story in Genesis, Chapter 1: 27. In this one, G-d has created a being that is both male and female. G-d then separates the two to create Adam and Eve. In short, the early rabbis thought that the two stories were contradictory and only taught the one about the rib. I see them as being constant. G-d created an androgynous being and then separated the two halves. In other words, man and woman were created at the same time."

"I never knew about the first story of creation. I am beginning to like you more. Too bad you're views will be lost when you leave the rabbinate."

"Ann, I won't ever leave the rabbinate. Once a rabbi, always a rabbi. And, I'll continue to teach and maybe, just maybe, finish my report to you if I may."

The rabbi contacted the second name on the list given to him by White Eagle. He phoned information and then called Joy Sanders. He asked if he could come over to her home and she grudgingly agreed. She lived on the reservation in a small yellow pre-fab house. Unlike Linda, Joy's name was not matched by her appearance. Her face was set in a frozen scowl. She was irate. It turned out the council had allocated some of the funds from the casino to build some low-cost housing. It was a way of showing the casino was making things better. Unfortunately, the workmanship was poor, materials cheap, and no one had bothered to check the soil. So, the homes were falling apart and sinking at funny angles. To say she was mad was an understatement. She spent a lot of time complaining about the cracks in the wall and how the people at the casino were trying to rip off the Antchu Nation.

It was hard for the rabbi to ask her the questions he wanted, so he decided to get a better understanding of why she blamed the casino for her house problems.

Her response was short and sweet. "The casino is making tons of money that we never see, so they sent a few pennies and poorly constructed buildings to make us be quiet and not ask questions."

He thought his visit had been a waste until Joy shared she had talked with Ruth a lot about the casino. Both of them strongly agreed with White Eagle that the casino would corrupt the children and the reservation itself. They felt that everyone was blinded by the potential money it could bring to the reservation. "That's why I went to work. I get a little better than minimum wage serving sandwiches to customers who just can't wait to give their money to the casino," admitted Joy. She continued, "Even Morning Breeze, who everyone respects almost as much as White Eagle, was finally convinced to support the casino because it was a way to get out of the White man's control." Joy was certain the casino was making a lot of money but that the reservation was seeing only a small amount of the proceeds. She felt that Ruth also believed there was something terribly wrong happening at the casino and that she got a job to uncover it. Joy concluded, "She was killed by the casino because she knew too much."

The rabbi had thought this conversation was going somewhere until Joy's conspiracy theory was revealed. While he did believe JFK was probably killed by more than one gunman, he was not inclined to believe general conspiracy theories. He really couldn't visualize the casino sending out hit men to kill Ruth while White Eagle was conveniently drunk enough so he could be framed. This seemed ridiculous. He hoped the third contact, if it could be made, might give him something to go on.

The third contact's name was Blossom. The rabbi's luck was holding. Blossom was at the casino and was willing to see the rabbi during her afternoon break. He expected to find a petite woman who also worked as a change girl. They met at an outdoor area that had tables and umbrellas, free from the smoke and the noise of the casino. It was a haven for the employees. She was sitting at a table near a large pine tree that, if one ignored the large casino, contributed a nice rustic flavor. She was well dressed-a no-nonsense person. He soon learned she had an advanced degree in accounting, was an astute bookkeeper and ran the computer records for the casino. Unlike Joy and Linda who were friends with Ruth before she went to work at the casino,

Ruth became friends with Blossom while on the job. Blossom shared that Ruth made a point of having lunch with her on a regular basis.

The rabbi was intrigued and concluded that Ruth was seeking out Blossom for reasons other than she was a nice person, pleasant and good-hearted. Ruth had a lot of friends and it would have been more natural to have lunch with Linda or Joy. Yet it would appear she went out of her way to get to know Blossom. He supposed there was a motive, and that motive had to do with Blossom's job.

So the rabbi decided to ask, "What did you two talk about?"

"All sorts of things. I was curious to hear about White Eagle and why she chose to marry him. She asked me about accounting and how the casino accounted for things. She told me she wanted to be an accountant. She really wanted to know what I did. Most people just don't care." The rabbi followed up her comments with detailed questions, which uncovered that Ruth wanted to know about the different type of checking accounts and how one could get through security to look at the books.

Ann stopped the rabbi with a question, "Had you heard that Ruth wanted to be an accountant?"

"No, I didn't hear any mention of it prior to Blossom's assertion. Either she kept this secret deep in her heart or she was lying to Blossom."

"Why would she lie?"

"To get information."

"Do you think Joy was right and men in black coats with white ties took Ruth out?" reflected Ann.

"Patience, patience. I had one more visit."

He also wanted to meet Morning Breeze, a good friend of Blue Star and White Eagle, who knew much about the casino since he was a member of the Tribal Council. He had called Morning Breeze earlier in the day at the Tribal

Council's office. Morning Breeze was not eager to meet him, which surprised the rabbi. They arranged to meet at the end of the day in the Council's office on the other side of the parking lot from the casino.

The rabbi remembered that they had first met at the sweat ceremony. Morning Breeze wasn't overly friendly. He was cordial, but there was no heart connection like he had that day with Blue Star and Carol. His office was nice-it had a very modern look to it. There was a thick green carpet, many Indian woven blankets and baskets on the walls, Navajo sand paintings on brown backgrounds with striking bright colors, and other beautiful paintings. He was young, in his mid-to-late forties, wearing fashionable wire-rim glasses. He was regarded as the young up-and-coming leader of the reservation. He looked at the rabbi with great suspicion. Before the rabbi could ask him any questions, he attacked first by asking the rabbi, "Why does a white man want to help the Owl Preservation and now White Eagle?"

141

Morning Breeze revealed he had only agreed to talk with the rabbi because the rabbi was trying to help White Eagle. He did not trust any White man, especially not one who said he was a "friend." Morning Breeze went on to say, 'All of our supposed friends eventually turned against us. We have no friends, just the tribe.' When the rabbi asked why he changed his vote on the casino, he almost spat the answer at the rabbi. "I agree with White Eagle that it's not the best way to make money, but you don't give us any choice. You keep us trapped in poverty on our reservations. I came to understand that a casino can give us money and money buys power. Now, you are afraid of us."

The rabbi didn't fully disagree with his righteous anger and this outburst seemed to be an echo of White Eagle's sentiments. When there is pain and injustice, there is rage and distrust. And yet, with White Eagle's absence, he was also taking on the role as the main spiritual leader for the tribe. Unlike White Eagle who was always outwardly friendly, Morning Breeze seemed to wear his anger as a badge of honor. The rabbi had no sense of a spiritual glow he always saw around White Eagle. He didn't think people survived on money or anger; there must be the deeper calling of the spirit. So, he decided to change the focus of the conversation and appeal to his spiritual side.

The rabbi reminded him he had put his glasses on the altar at his first sweat and the rabbi knew that he was a deeply spiritual man. He explained that it was critical to hold onto their traditions. Morning Breeze proudly told the rabbi how he went in search of eagle feathers to give to those who do ceremonies and that he often helped elders, such as Blue Star and White Eagle, conduct ceremonies. He told Rabbi Daniels the reservation was in a great turmoil over Ruth's death and people were coming to him to perform the ceremonies that White Eagle had previously conducted. He was worried because White Eagle had become a role model to so many of the children. Now, many would give up hope. He had to maintain the people's dignity and strength.

Morning Breeze had calmed down and the conversation had become cordial, so he offered the rabbi a Diet Coke and some pistachios. Morning Breeze reminisced about Ruth and how he liked her very much, even though she was not an Indian. He believed she had made the right decision to go to work at the casino. He was obviously proud the casino was able to offer employment to virtually anyone on the reservation who wanted to work. He concluded, saying, "White Eagle should have seen what good this casino is doing. If he had, maybe Ruth would still be alive today."

Chapter 10
Questions

The fool wonders, the wise man asks.
Disraeli

143

It was Wednesday morning, and Ann was feeling particularly sad. She had found herself in the empty rabbi's study. She liked the rabbi's old roll top desk filled with papers that appeared to be placed at random. Nevertheless, she knew the rabbi could, almost by instinct, put his hand down and come out of this mess with the exact paper he was looking for. She had tried to organize him only to realize that he was organized - in this disorganized fashion. She lovingly trolled her hand among his books. He had more books than any other person she had met. One bookcase was devoted to history, philosophy, spirituality. Another contained books on the Holocaust and Israel. There was an entire bookcase with various prayer books from different Jewish traditions and covering all the holidays. The largest collection appeared to be various Bibles and commentaries. It seemed to her that there were commentaries on the commentaries. Of course, there were the legal texts-the Mishnah, Talmud, and later legal codes. She smiled as she came across a whole row of stories, folklore and humor. She wasn't surprised when she saw the large collection of Muslim, Christian, Buddhist, and Hindu books as well as books about other religions. She wondered if he had read all these books. She wondered if she would leave when he left.

Rabbi Daniels came in a little out of breath. "Sorry, I was busy telling the pre-school children a story about the runaway challah. You see, in the story they forget the tradition of covering the challah and it runs away."

"It must have some very short legs," said Ann smiling.

"You told me there was a message from White Eagle?"

"Yes, he says it's urgent and you should see him right away," Ann reported.

"Are there problems at the jail? I've been afraid some of the other inmates were going to treat him roughly," said the rabbi, in an agitated voice.

"He didn't say. Maybe he remembered something. Maybe he wants to confess," Ann added. After the rabbi had reported his conversations at the reservation, she was becoming convinced he had in fact killed his wife. She thought the rabbi, for his own needs, was becoming a little obsessed with saving White Eagle. He had this savior fixation. Wasn't he in the wrong religion then?

There was a school budget meeting he could not miss. The meeting seemed interminable, but it finally ended with the clear message that the rabbi should be doing more to raise money. The rabbi had not wanted to be the one who was always asking for donations. He was often reminded other rabbis did raise money for their congregations. At this meeting, they again needled him as they listed their requirements for new books, more school supplies, maintenance on the aging building, and additional scholarships. And since education was so important to the rabbi, one board member suggested the rabbi should spend a little more time socializing with certain people and, when the time was right, ask them to support "the future leaders of the Jewish people." One member of the committee, Tony, who was not the rabbi's biggest supporter, had to throw in his own pet agenda: perhaps if the rabbi's sermons were more contemporary and less scholarly, more people would attend services. Normally the rabbi would be hurt, but he reasoned that soon he would be gone so why get into a fight with Tony. This would not be his problem in a short time, so why worry?

He rushed out of the meeting with quick good byes. He even shook Tony's hand, thanking him for his positive comments, which left Tony confused and speechless.

Rabbi Daniels arrived at the jail after pressing his luck by going faster than the posted speed, as well as going through a few lights that could arguably have been considered to have already turned red. Tom Singer was waiting for him and did not look relaxed.

"Rabbi, White Eagle is usually so calm. He called for me late yesterday and demanded to see you as soon as possible. He is excited about something.

He stated he had to give you something personally. You're going to meet him in the conference room. I need to be with you and make sure nothing inappropriate is taking place. As a friend, I need to remind you that you are not his attorney and I'm not sure you would qualify as his rabbi. I'm not a lawyer, but I do want to warn you anything I see or hear I will be forced to repeat in court. So, if he confesses to you and I hear it, I'll have to testify to what is said. Be careful and don't let him say too much. He is probably in the conference room right now."

He followed Tom through the metal barriers into the familiar room where White Eagle had performed his healing ritual. He saw another police officer leaning against the far wall and White Eagle seated on a chair behind a plain table with an empty chair across from him.

When he entered, White Eagle stood again. The rabbi felt honored. But, this was a different White Eagle. He was standing straight and he looked strong. The rabbi didn't say anything but sat in the empty chair. When White Eagle sat down, his eyes totally focused on the rabbi. White Eagle made no small talk. It was obvious he was preoccupied. Whatever was going to happen next the rabbi knew was going to be important. White Eagle had brought his medicine bundle. Was he going to perform another ritual, the rabbi wondered? Without speaking, the elder opened up his medicine bundle and took everything out. He then lifted up the seemingly empty leather wrapping and showed the rabbi that there was a torn lining. He put his finger under the lining and extracted two pieces of paper. He carefully handed the first one to the rabbi. The first piece of paper was yellowed by time and the edges were torn. It was a hand-drawn map, obviously old but of no immediate relevance, at least that the rabbi could tell. He then gave the rabbi the second piece of paper, which appeared to be a listing of checks from some record book. There were recent dates, check numbers, notations, and amounts. The rabbi looked up at White Eagle, his face a full-formed question mark.

White Eagle looked back for a moment, and then declared, "These papers are not mine." Since the rabbi did not respond, he repeated, "These papers are not mine, I did not put them here." He emphasized by pointing to his pouch. He then took the map from the rabbi and said "This looks like an old map made by a military surveying team of the area that became our reservation. I have never seen this map before. I have no idea about this other page. But someone put them in my pouch."

"What do you mean?" the rabbi asked, not grasping the reason White Eagle saw such importance in this discovery.

"I know my medicine bag, it is part of me. These papers were not there before. Someone intentionally placed them in the bag."

"Do you think they are connected to Ruth's death?"

White Eagle had no idea. But the rabbi thought there were two people who could possibly help him find out. He returned to the synagogue and over the course of a break reported to Ann about the latest developments. Ann was not impressed and was worried the rabbi was getting too involved for his own good. On the other hand, and she had to be honest, she was curious. And, just maybe White Eagle was not guilty. He gave the originals to Ann and asked her to put them in a safe place after making several copies.

The rabbi returned to his car and made the now-familiar drive to the casino. He arrived in the afternoon. The parking lot was already crowded. Unlike the hotels in Vegas, this casino was modest. No huge sign announced a gala show or a cheap buffet. He had only been inside briefly to find Linda and he didn't like it. The cars waiting for their occupants to return were not luxury cars as he remembered seeing parked in front of the Vegas casinos. Rather, Hondas, Fords, and Chevy's were the main occupants of the parking spaces. There were a few BMW's and Mercedes, but they were the exception and not the rule.

He took off his *kippah* and put on an old gray canvas floppy hat he kept in the car in case it rained. It wasn't very flattering, but it did the trick. He usually wore a *kippah* unless he was playing sports, sleeping, taking a shower, or just wanted to blend in. Sometimes his sons asked him to wear a hat rather than a *kippah*. While they were proud their father was a rabbi, they often didn't like the extra attention his *kippah* often drew. And this time, the rabbi wanted to be less conspicuous. He had decided he wanted to get a better feel for the place and didn't want too many people to know he was looking over the casino.

He went through the open doors and was immediately hit by the thick cloud of black smoke. He gagged. His eyes adjusted. He again saw the banks of slot machines with people mechanically putting in coin after coin. It seemed they didn't care if they won or lost. Their hand just went down to the silver trays and up to the slot for the coin. It looked like human machines feeding metal machines. To his left was a card room with blackjack and poker tables. Here, at least, people talked to each other. Further down the room were long tables filled with people, many seniors, playing bingo. There were no fancy or cheap restaurants to attract the gambler, just a small snack area. Joy was behind the counter. He waved at her and she hesitantly waved back. She didn't seem happy about something and then it hit him. She was the woman at the sweat who had told Sue White women should leave their men alone. She would have been upset Ruth had married White Eagle. How upset could she have been, he wondered.

Two more things now struck him. Most of the workers in the casino were not Native Americans. Moreover, he was shocked by the many sacred Indian symbols painted on the sides of the gambling hall as decorations. These were ritual symbols like salamanders, the sun, eagles, coyotes and the rainbow. There were elaborate sun circles. It looked to him as if they were desecrating their heritage in an attempt to create an "authentic" Indian atmosphere for the tourists. For the rabbi, this display of ritual objects would be like putting a cross or the Star of David on the wall to endorse or bless the gamblers. He felt soiled and thought he should probably find some sage to smudge himself with when he left.

He saw Blossom walking across the room and went quickly in her direction. However, he heard his name being called, "Rabbi Daniels, it's interesting to see you here." It was clearly an awkward moment. The voice belonged to a member of his ritual committee, Julie Silverman. As he agonizingly turned with his smile quickly painted on, he saw not only her husband Brad but a few other congregants as well. Clearly, this was a group of friends who had come to gamble for the day. They all looked at the rabbi and it was obvious they were thinking he should not be at the casino. At that instant he had to control a laugh that wanted to escape from his throat as he was reminded of a joke about a rabbi who had wanted to eat ham his whole life. Finally, he could not contain himself anymore and drove to a town far away. He made sure there was absolutely no one he knew and felt if he were going to violate the laws of *kashrut*, he would do it right. He ordered a whole pig, complete with a baked apple in its mouth. As the rabbi was waiting, it happened that the president of his congregation entered the restaurant and, upon seeing the rabbi, walked over. Out of the corner of his eye, the Rabbi saw the pig making its way to his table. When the plate was placed in front of the rabbi, he exclaimed to the astonished president, "Look what happened, I ordered a baked apple and see how they serve it."

With the joke in mind, Rabbi Daniels went over to this group knowing full well they would spread it all over the congregation that he took time off in the middle of the day to go to the casino dressed incognito. Also, the rumors about him and Ann, when added to his being in a casino, would add to a rather negative view of their rabbi. He knew he had to say something. He just didn't know what to say. Suddenly he heard Blossom's voice, "Rabbi, did you have more questions to ask me about Ruth's murder?"

He instantly answered more loudly than he should have, "Yes, do you have a few minutes?" The rabbi paused to make a silent prayer: "Thank you G-d." He quickly looked at the Silverman's and the rest of their group "How are you all? I need to hurry, but I look forward to seeing you this Friday night at services."

Julie opened her mouth as if to say something and the rabbi deliberately turned his back and hurried over toward Blossom. "Could we talk for a few minutes alone?" She looked at her watch. "Yes, I have a fifteen minute break I can take now." She led him to the back area where they had previously talked.

"This is where Ruth and I often ate," she announced as she looked around. "Usually there are squirrels that we would feed with some bread from our sandwiches. I miss her."

The rabbi took out a Xerox copy of the page listing the checks White Eagle had given him. There were ten checks listed. Most appeared to be for office supplies, a car repair, and a large $10,000 payment to a B&M corporation. Blossom took the page and looked over it carefully. "Where did you get this?" she asked.

The rabbi instantly knew this was from the casino. He decided to be partially honest and told her how White Eagle found the paper in his medicine pouch. He asked if she could tell him anything about the ledger page. She told him the format resembled the system they had in the casino. She looked around to make sure that no one was looking and told him she thought this was from the check record controlled by the manager of the casino. Blossom took care of payroll and knew most of the daily expenses. However, while she knew the manager's account existed, she was never allowed to see it. As Blossom was talking, a smile suddenly spread across her face. She looked around again and announced in a very confidential voice, "Ruth got this, didn't she?"

149

Blossom told the rabbi how she had explained the various accounting records to Ruth and that there was this secret one. She had been excited about this information. Ruth had asked her if she knew how to get past the security code and get into the account. Well, one night when Blossom was working late, she did come across a scrap of paper left by the manager, which contained the code. She kept that paper thinking that one day she would browse around. When she told Ruth that she had the code, Ruth told her she should give her a copy of the code just in case Blossom lost the original. Ruth had promised to keep it safe.

When the rabbi asked Blossom if anything seemed unusual about the account, she was upset but not surprised the manager had spent money to repair his own car, which was not used for casino business. She had never heard of the B&M Corporation, which she thought was strange as she knew or at least thought she knew all the companies that did business with the casino.

They talked for a little while longer before she had to leave when her break was over. She had barely left when a powerfully built and intense man with a serious face sat down in the spot just vacated by Blossom. The man was in his mid fifties; his long black hair was tied back with a leather thong. The rabbi actually felt a little uncomfortable, even threatened. The man placed his large hands, with turquoise and silver rings on several fingers, on the table and gazed at the rabbi.

"Hello, Rabbi Daniels," he began. "I am Mike Tall Horse, the manager of the casino. I know you're helping White Eagle. It was a terrible thing. I liked Ruth. Is there any way I can help you?"

Rabbi Daniels coughed; he was now seriously thinking of Joy's conspiracy theory and looked to see if there was anyone else around. He relaxed a little when he saw a few other employees casually talking at a nearby table.

He was still nervous but had enough presence of mind to ask about the sacred drawings on the walls of the casino. The manager didn't seem to mind the somewhat pointed question and told him they didn't want to follow the Vegas model. They wanted to make a statement to all who came in that they were guests of the Antchu people. At the same time, they wanted to honor the tradition. They had asked one of the elders to tell them which symbols they could publicly use and he had given his approval. Rabbi Daniels next inquired about the number of Native Americans employed. Mike, this time seemingly a little annoyed, shared that there were some four hundred employees and around fifty were from the reservation. While the number might seem small, he boasted there was no longer any unemployment on the reservation for anyone who wanted to work. He did admit most of the management positions weren't people from the reservation. "Ruth took a job of providing change and cleaning up the offices in the back, a position she requested," he uttered defensively.

The rabbi, now feeling more confident and still aware there were people in the patio area, asked, "How much does the casino contribute to drinking and crime on the reservation?"

Mike's agitation increased. "It's no secret there's a major drinking problem on this and other reservations. The problem was here before we came. However, people drink from hopelessness. I believe there's less drinking now as we're giving people work. We provide jobs where there were none. We hope to provide college scholarships and training programs. And, any employee who has a drinking or drug problem is given money for a rehab program."

The rabbi thought to himself, "Is he serious?" Giving out and legitimizing booze, which is a part of the gambling scene, does not seem a sound method of providing a way to solve a chronic drinking problem. This guy was selling a whole suitcase of goods. Only fifty employees are from the tribe. And probably those are mostly the menial jobs. Who do they think they're helping?

Rabbi Daniels then asked about the television commercials that encouraged people to come to the casino by suggesting that gambling was a significant part of the Antchu culture. "Don't you think you are adding yet another negative stereotype that may demean your people, your culture?"

The battle of words between them continued. "In truth, gambling and games of chance were always part of our culture. We show our commercials to our elders. If they thought we were being unfair to our heritage, they would tell us. Perhaps they know better what is demeaning than you do."

The rabbi now aimed at his real target. "Who really gets the lion's share of the profit from the casino's operations?" 151

"Rabbi," Mike began unhurriedly, "I could take offense to that question and the other questions you've been asking, but I won't. There are always allegations of nefarious connections like the Mafia. There has never been any proof, just allegations by those who are jealous of our success and power. Everyone wants to close us down. The card parlors, casino owners in Vegas, even the governor. But they can't. We can afford the best lawyers and no one can stop us. Let me tell you we run this casino for the benefit of our people. If we could make money another way we would. But, we can't. And the money we make is used to help build new housing, roads, set up scholarship funds, support powwows and educational programs, and build that beautiful conference and council meeting complex on the other side of this parking lot. We poor, deprived Indians, even give to some charitable organizations in the community. Can you imagine, all those people who looked down on us for so long now come to us for help?" He paused for a moment and then his dark eyes locked onto Rabbi Daniels' eyes. "I thought you were helping White Eagle? Why all these questions about the casino?"

"I am here to both help White Eagle and the community. I care about social responsibility and I care what happens to people. I agree with White Eagle's concerns about the casino as a dangerous and negative influence on the reservation. And, since White Eagle started to get drunk after Ruth came to work here, I wanted to find out more."

The manager pursed his lips and nodded slightly, "White Eagle is our grandfather and I respect him very much. But even Morning Breeze, who was first against us, came around to understand the casino could be the key to the survival of the reservation. I am proud we have a casino and I resent you and those like you who want to tell us what we should do." He lowered his voice and pointed his finger at the rabbi, "Now that I've answered your questions, I hope you will leave my staff alone and not come back here unless you want to gamble. And, if you are as smart as I think you are, you'll leave now."

The rabbi noticed all the rings. "When you were talking to Blue Star at the preservation, what was all that about?"

Mike had stood to his full height while the rabbi was talking. "Your good manners were left at home I see. For your information, your friend Blue Star borrowed money from our casino to build his Preservation, which he has neglected to pay back. And just so you don't get your back up, we aren't charging any interest. But, he does owe us the money and he will pay." With that, he stood up and walked away, leaving the rabbi a little shaken and wet from perspiration. He truly felt scared and watched his rear view mirror as he left the parking lot to drive home.

"Well, I vote for this man or someone working for him as the prime suspect," Ann declared.

The rabbi stood up from his chair and walked over to the shelf filled with the tall red books of the Talmud. "Ann, as I read and try to understand our tradition, I am often struck by how each person is formed by their experiences and how they attempt to make sense of the world in their own way. And so, I often just stand in awe of the uniqueness of the individual spirit. A famous rabbi, Hillel, taught, 'Do not judge another until you are in his position.' Hillel also wrote, 'If I am not for myself, who will be for me. If I am only for myself, what am I.'" The rabbi looked at Ann and in a somewhat somber voice revealed, "I think I'm in over my head, a little scared, and not quite sure what to do next."

Chapter 11
The Dilemma

Better is the end of a thing than its beginning.
Ecclesesiates 7.8

153

The outdoor chapel was behind the synagogue and down a winding concrete path. Next door was the noisy preschool filled with small children. There was a wood play structure with ladders, slides, and swings that was near the entry to the chapel as if such proximity were a reminder that children were a critical part of this community. The rabbi had called Sue Miller to join him for their regular meeting in this place that often served as his personal sanctuary. He liked the oak trees that surrounded the chapel, forming a canopy. He was walking around the grassy area between the wooden gazebo that formed the raised podium and the concrete seats when he noticed Sue at the entrance to the chapel.

"Thank you for meeting me out here. I feel like I can breathe here away from the phone, the computer, the noise," she said. Sue was wearing a white blouse, faded blue jeans and dirty white tennis shoes, a stark contrast to the rabbi's black pants, white shirt, navy blue tie, and blue and white *kippah* on his head. "Do you like our chapel?" he asked.

"It seems cold. Too much concrete."

"We put cushions on top of the steps. It makes it easier to sit during our summer services."

Sue walked down the steps to join the rabbi on the grassy area as he continued. "I like the chapel. I like the green of the grass and the gray of the oak trees behind me." He raised his hands and pointed to a grove of trees to his right. "I also like being near those fruit trees. There is an apple, orange, and peach tree. They were planted to honor someone who had died. When I bring the preschool children out here and pick a fruit, I tell them about that person. It is as if the memory of that person is like the fruit, always ripening and nourishing." There was silence for awhile. "I may not be able to finish teaching you. Have you heard the rumors?"

"Which ones? You are a popular topic of conversation these days."

"The ones about my leaving. Most people have been very supportive, but there are some who are disappointed. They feel deserted and forsaken. I'm not sure if I feel sorrier for myself or for them."

Sue had been quietly watching the rabbi. "Rabbi, not only are all beginnings hard, so are all endings. You've been important to these people and their anger mirrors their inner pain at losing you. If they didn't care, they wouldn't be upset. You're a unique rabbi; you have truly been a teacher, not just a religious leader. You've planted seeds that will continue to grow and sprout. Perhaps your work here is finished. Maybe you have new work to do."

"Perhaps," was all the Rabbi answered. There was silence again. "What do you want to study today?"

"Well, I'd like to know a little about the Talmud. I've heard this term a lot. What is it?"

"That's a good topic for today. The Talmud is a group of books. They contain stories and debates between some of our greatest rabbis. These texts also contain some wonderful principles of legal reasoning."

The rabbi could tell this was not going to be easy. "Let me use the American legal system to explain our Jewish legal structure. There is the U.S. constitution and then various court cases that apply the general principles to specific situations. So, take the right to a free attorney in a criminal case. The constitution does not actually say one gets a free attorney. But in the sixties, the Supreme Court effectively ruled the legal system had become so complex it was unfair for a scared, untrained defendant to go against a highly skilled and experienced prosecutor. Similarly, we have records of rabbis acting like judges discussing various cases in an attempt to apply the general Biblical rules in day-to-day situations. The first record of this debate is called the Mishnah, which was written down around 250 of the Common Era. The Talmud, much more detailed, was codified around 500 C.E. I love studying these codes. It's as if I'm going back in time and sitting on a bench listening to these great rabbis debate legal points to make our tradition vital to the lives of ordinary people. And, it has these wonderful principles of logic."

The rabbi put his hands behind his back and resumed pacing on the grass, seemingly oblivious to Sue's presence. He had entered his own world. His blue tie swung like a pendulum, side to side. "There are two opposing legal principles taught by Rabbi Ishmael to help understand the Talmud. One is called *cal la'prat* and the other, its twin, *prat'la col*. The first one is to get a general principle from which particulars follow and its antithesis is to go from the particulars to the general."

He stopped pacing and now faced Sue. His eyes were wide as if something had just dawned on him. "I know Ann's been filling you in on all the stuff with White Eagle. I felt that the police had developed a general concept that White Eagle had killed Ruth in a drunken rage. They made all the particular facts conform to this view. And, to be honest, most of the facts did support this theory. However, I am disturbed there were little pieces that didn't fit that puzzle."

The rabbi's conversational voice had now changed to that of the teacher. "Let's review the evidence using these Talmudic principles, from the particulars first and then see what type of general thesis might develop.

"First, there is the errant bullet shell. For the police, the shell did not fall along their prescribed pattern. So, they concluded that either it was kicked or it bounced to get to its position near the bookcase. Let us presume it fell exactly where the gun had been fired. If that was true, then the bullet hole above the door frame makes perfect sense."

"I'm lost. Someone fired at the door frame?" asked Sue.

Rabbi Daniels stopped and turned towards her, "No, someone was firing at someone in the door frame and either wanted to scare them or missed." He continued his orbital movement as if a professor lecturing to a class. "Next, the police believed White Eagle started shooting as he moved towards Ruth. That pattern could just as easily be made by someone shooting at Ruth and then moving away, back towards the sleeping White Eagle."

He looked up expectantly at Sue. "Do you see, there are many possibilities for what occurred beyond the general theory adopted by the police."

He continued both his thoughts and his ambling "Then there was the eagle feather." His right forefinger began to stab the air. "They thought it had been unintentionally damaged in the fall. What if it had intentionally been broken?"

He turned full body to Sue with his jacket open and stared at her.

Staring right back, she confessed, "I'm still lost. What about the ledger page and map you told me about?"

"Ah, you see, then," the rabbi concluded triumphantly.

"No, I don't see." Again, Sue was staring at him in utter confusion.

The rabbi stopped moving abruptly, "Yes! You've been a great help." He ran up the stairs of the chapel towards the parking lot. As an afterthought, he stopped at the top of the steps and turned, "Sorry, I need to run. I'll see you next week." Sue just sat there, bewildered.

The rabbi drove to the sheriff's office in downtown St. Luke's looking for Detective Markman. After the rabbi waited for what seemed like a long time, Detective Markman came down the stairs to the lobby. They walked over to a bench in the lobby of the brightly lit rectangle room that was surprisingly empty. Perhaps there wasn't much crime in St. Luke's, the rabbi thought, except for the occasional murder. The rabbi explained his theory. He feared the detective would throw him out on his ear. The detective raised many objections and concluded the theory had "more holes then a spaghetti strainer." Nevertheless, he was a little curious and was willing to gather the information requested by the rabbi.

When Rabbi Daniels returned to the synagogue, Ann tried to find out what had happened. "That was quite a show you put on for Sue. She told me how you played the role of the absent- minded professor and then ran out. Sue's impression by what you were saying before you ran is that you know who killed Ruth and it wasn't White Eagle."

The rabbi didn't take the bait. He sat mutely, staring at his book of Jewish stories. He would soon be teaching a class at the religious school and loved sparking their attention with a good story. Ann was not deterred. "By the way, our alleged affair is no longer the talk of the town. The new rumor on the hit parade is you have resigned because you have gone native-Native American that is. Your little secret visit to the casino is no longer so secret."

The rabbi was truly shocked. He had always done the right thing. In college he avoided taking drugs because he wanted to run for public office and didn't want a past that could be brought up to bite him. He only got drunk once in college when he was challenged to a drinking contest on a school field trip. He felt trapped and agreed to drink. He won, only to throw up in front of everyone a short time later. He acknowledged he was so worried about how others saw him that he had missed out on some aspects of life. And now he had been accused of having an affair with his older secretary, not being a good rabbi because he didn't raise money, and skulking around as a wanna-be Indian. He presumed his reputation would now be permanently ruined. These depressing thoughts were interrupted by Ann calling to him through the door, "Detective Markman."

The rabbi picked up the phone and after a few pleasantries, the detective reported, "They rushed this through as a favor to me. The results have come back and you're right. However, we both know there's not enough here to free White Eagle or charge someone else."

The rabbi had anticipated this reaction and asked the detective if he was willing to trust him. The rabbi then told the detective his plan.

"Hey, it's your neck and your reputation. Remember, I will just be passing by. I don't mind watching. It will be interesting any way it goes. But, if it goes badly, and I think it may, I'll have to arrest you. It will make the front page. You may also get sued."

The rabbi didn't think he had much of a reputation to lose and his future was already in doubt. Why not make his humiliation complete with his arrest. The potential lawsuit was also a very real possibility, he knew. The cost of the suit in terms of money, time and psychic energy were tremendous. As he thought about the effect on his kids, he almost called back the detective, to cancel his plans.

Ann came into his office without knocking, "So, are you going to do it?" She had obviously been listening.

"You could be arrested for eavesdropping on an official phone call."

"What are they going to do? I'm an old defenseless woman."

"My heart is bleeding cold borscht," the rabbi bantered back. "I don't know if it will work."

"Come on, don't give me that 'I'm not sure stuff.' You're in too deep. Can I come along?"

"No, absolutely not. Someone has to keep the temple together." As if in an afterthought he said, "Someone has to bail me out."

A few minutes later, the rabbi was driving yet again but perhaps for the last time to the reservation. He looked out the window at the passing green chaparral and white rocks as he wound up the mountain pass. The lake looked particularly blue this morning and his heart seemed to pause a little as he passed the turnoff for the spot that hosted the powwow. He drove in silence. He kept going over what he would say. How does one accuse another human being of being a murderer?

He finally passed the casino and drove up the hill into the residential area, but didn't find who he was looking for. He came back down and wasn't sure if he should try the casino or the council building. He decided that the best bet was the council building. His legs started shaking. He had never known this level of panic and fear. He wasn't even sure he could speak. He parked the car in front of the wood and glass structure. Was there anyone he knew there? There, at one of the tables talking with a few people sat Morning Breeze.

He got out of the car and waited nervously for the conversation to end and the men to leave. He then entered the building through a glass door at the side.

Morning Breeze looked up at his approach. He studied the rabbi in silence. Rabbi Daniels sat across from him. "I have a few more questions for you." He placed a plain brown paper bag on the table in front of Morning Breeze. He reached in and took out the crumpled eagle feather that had been at the base of the bookcase and placed it on the table. He then put the paper bag on the floor next to him, "Do you recognize this eagle feather?"

"Yes, I gave this eagle feather to grandfather White Eagle. What happened to it?"

"It is my guess that Ruth, before she died, broke the feather as a message. What do you think that message might be?"

"How should I know?" he said, his voice was rising.

"Interesting that she choose to break this sacred object just before she died," the rabbi calmly stated.

"Rabbi, you don't know that for sure. If you've asked your questions..."

Before he could finish, the rabbi picked up the bag from the floor and again placed it on the table. He deliberately reached inside and took out a copy of the map, "Do you recognize this?"

Morning Breeze took the Xerox copy and stared at it for a moment, "No, what is it?"

"That's strange. Your fingerprints are on the original."

With that comment, Morning Breeze's head jerked up. The rabbi reached into the paper bag again and withdrew another piece of paper. "This is a copy of a check record from the manager's account over at the casino. Please notice the circled item, a check for $10,000 to B&M Corporation. I checked out that corporation and it turns out you are the president, the only board member and the sole shareholder. Why would the casino be giving you $10,000?"

Morning Breeze almost grabbed the sheet from the rabbi's hands. "I am a consultant to them on Native American traditions."

"Oh, you're the one who reviews the casino's commercials or if it's appropriate to put sacred objects around the gambling hall. Is that how you earned this ten thousand dollars?"

"Yes," he replied.

"Then this ten thousand dollar is compensation. I'm sure the casino has filed the proper tax forms, issued you a 1099, and you've declared this amount on your taxes?"

"Don't be a fool, Rabbi!"

"Have you gotten a lot more money from the casino for your consulting work?"

"A little."

Rabbi Daniels pulled another piece of white paper from the paper bag. "This is a record of your deposits for the past two years. It shows monthly payments of $10,000. You must work very hard for the casino to earn this type of money. I find it strange you should get so much, don't you?" He then looked directly into Morning Breeze's cold black eyes, "It seems more like a payoff for something."

"If that is all," said Morning Breeze. He backed his chair away from the table in an effort to leave, but he was mesmerized by the rabbi's hand going into the bag once again, where he removed a gun and a shell and placed them squarely on the table.

"There are these two items. I know that you didn't intend to kill Ruth."

Morning Breeze just stared at the rabbi as he continued, "When you came in the door, she fired the gun at you. What were you after? This!" He then pointed to the copy of the map he had previously put on the table.

At this point the rabbi had hoped Morning Breeze was going to confess. It always worked in the movies. But Morning Breeze still sat calmly with a smirk spreading across his face. Well, so much for his theory. Maybe it was okay that Detective Markman hadn't shown up as planned. But he had one more item and he was praying this one would work.

He then put his hand one last time in the bag and took out a black piece of plastic. "I notice you have a nice new pair of wire-rim glasses. But, at the sweat, the glasses you placed on the altar had a black frame, just like this piece that was found at the murder scene. And, just like the map, it has your fingerprints as well."

The rabbi first noticed the eyes-Morning Breezes' had lost their focus. Then a strange sneer began to spread over his face. The fear that suddenly erupted in the rabbi's body and made him want to run did not prepare him. The lunge Morning Breeze made at the rabbi caught him off guard. He didn't even have time to put up his hands to ward off the attack.

Just as suddenly, Morning Breeze was gone. It took a moment for the rabbi to realize Morning Breeze was face down on the floor with Detective Markman over him. Morning Breeze struggled for an instant, but then his body seemed to crumble as the handcuffs were applied to his wrists that were now behind his back.

The rabbi was enjoying talking to Ann. He was in his favorite captain's chair in front of his roll top desk.

"Yes, Morning Breeze later confessed to killing Ruth and claimed it was an accident."

"Was Markman hiding and just sprung out at the right time?" she asked.

"Actually, no. We had planned to meet at Morning Breeze's home. He got there after I left and presumed I had not yet arrived. He waited for a while and then decided to look for me. He spotted me in the council office and was just coming in when Morning Breeze sprang."

"You were lucky. While I think you're a great guy, I have to be honest. That would not have been much of a contest."

"Thanks for the confidence."

"But, how did he know she had the map?"

"Detective Markman told me Morning Breeze described how he had come home and found Ruth looking through some of his papers in a desk drawer. She ran out and drove away when he came in. He looked through the papers and knew she had the map, so he followed her to her trailer to get it back. As he entered, she shot at him and he ran to get the gun from her. It went off in the struggle. She was killed. Then, he noticed White Eagle hadn't moved and realized that he was dead drunk. He quickly thought of a way to implicate White Eagle and hide the fact that Ruth had fired first. He wanted to make it look as if White Eagle, in a drunken rage, had been firing at Ruth. He took the gun and fired randomly at the wall walking backwards toward White Eagle. After wiping off the gun, he took a napkin and held the gun as he put it in White Eagle's hand, shot once more and let it fall to the floor, now with White Eagle's fingerprints."

"That makes sense," concluded Ann. "How come no-one heard the shots? Guns make a lot of noise."

"When I went to the trailer that day, I remember feeling that the trailer was isolated and that the noise of the freeway would have made it hard for me to sleep. I'm a very light sleeper. Probably those two factors combined to mask the noise."

"Wait, I have a lot more questions. How did Ruth get the ledger page, how did that lead to Morning Breeze, and what is the map all about?"

The rabbi was excited and replied rapidly, "It turned out Ruth probably had gone to work at the casino to play detective in an attempt to validate her husband's concerns. She learned how to break into the manager's money account from Blossom and must have printed out the page showing the bank payments. I don't know how she figured out that the B&M Company was

161

tied to Morning Breeze. I figured it out due to my love of movies. I remembered reading about the computer named 'Hal' in the 2001 a Space Odyssey. According to the article, 'Hal' stood for 'IBM.'"

Ann raised her hand and in a mock tone said, "Teacher, teacher, I still don't get it."

Rabbi Daniels deepened his voice, "Well, class," as he turned to write on an imaginary blackboard, "the first letter after H is I, the first letter after A is B and the first letter after L is M-IBM.'" He turned back to face Ann. "I thought -- what could B&M stand for? I added and subtracted letters and then just reversed them to make M&B. I instantly thought of Morning Breeze. Then the broken eagle feather which Morning Breeze had given to White Eagle but wasn't in the pouch again pointed to Morning Breeze."

"Why didn't Ruth just leave a note? Why the broken feather?"

"That troubled me for a long time. It was a strange way to leave a message, unless that was her only option. Don't forget the bullet casing near the items that fell from the top of the bookshelf and the bullet hole near the door. My guess is that Ruth knew Morning Breeze had seen her and was going to come after her. She went home figuring White Eagle would be there. When she saw him drunk, she panicked and remembered the gun on the top shelf. In her haste to get the gun, the other items from the top shelf fell down, the pipe, drum and the medicine pouch."

"Wait, the medicine pouch wasn't found on the floor, only the feather," Ruth objected.

"Exactly! The medicine pouch was found where it should not have been, on the second shelf. Ruth must have seen the pouch, taken the map and the ledger page and put them inside knowing that Morning Breeze would never look inside someone else's pouch and White Eagle would discover the papers. As she opened the pouch, she saw the feather she knew came from Morning Breeze and either out of anger or to leave a message broke it and left it on the floor. She put the medicine pouch on the second shelf and then tried to either kill or scare Morning Breeze as he entered."

"What about the black piece from the glasses? How did you tie that to Morning Breeze?"

"I remembered the sweat and that Morning Breeze had put his glasses on the altar. I checked and found out neither White Eagle nor Ruth wore glasses and Morning Breeze was now wearing wire-rim glasses. I presumed that in the struggle his glasses came off and got broken. When he picked up his glasses in his haste, he didn't notice that a piece was missing or didn't see the piece amongst all the stuff on the floor."

"And," added Ann, "there were his fingerprints on the broken glasses."

"Well, not exactly."

"You lied! Rabbis aren't supposed to lie."

"Well, the Talmud talks about a bride who is not so attractive. What should a rabbi say if questioned about the beauty of the bride? They conclude the appropriate thing to say is all brides are beautiful. So, I bluffed."

"A white lie. You're tricky, and I'm going to miss you," Ann didn't plan for that last remark to escape her lips. This was becoming a dangerous habit. She stammered to ask another question immediately, "But why was the map so important and why was Morning Breeze getting so much money?"

"There is an old Talmudic saying, 'Don't look at what someone says, look at what they do.' For many, Morning Breeze was a spiritual leader who was doing things to benefit the community. But what if his real goal was taking care of himself at any cost? Remember how I felt the spiritual symbols in the casino and the commercials were inappropriate and the casino manager had told me that they had been approved by an elder? I guessed the elder was Morning Breeze who, by these actions, suggested to me he was not a true protector of the tradition. Elders of the Native Americans take their symbols very seriously. If Morning Breeze was willing to sell out these traditions, what else was he willing to do? I don't know if Ruth knew about the map or was just on a fishing trip when she was going through Morning Breeze's papers the night of her murder, but that map is of the reservation area. I've showed it now to several people. No one had seen it before nor had any idea why it was so important."

"So, you still don't know why the map cost Ruth her life."

"That's not totally true. I have a guess. Remember when your car broke down and we found that retreat house? I've been thinking about that house and those rocks. So, I went to show the map again to White Eagle."

White Eagle had been released immediately when Morning Breeze had confessed. He didn't want to return to his trailer and was staying with Blue Star. Blue Star and the rabbi had been in communication through Gus' bar.

The next day, White Eagle entered the rabbi's study along with Blue Star and Carol. The rabbi invited Ann since she, in so many ways, had become integral to the whole episode. White Eagle had a lot of questions. Mostly he had a hard time accepting the fact that this friend, whom he had taught so much, could have taken money from the casino to change his vote, taken someone's life, and was also willing to frame him.

White Eagle finally understood Morning Breeze wanted the power and the honor of being an elder, but did not really understand the sacred obligation he was undertaking. White Eagle wasn't angry. He was sad. He was a remarkable man and the rabbi truly felt he was in the presence of a deeply spiritual human being. Then the rabbi stood up and crossed over to White Eagle. "I have a question for you. Please look again at the map that was in your medicine bag. No one understands why it was so important, yet it must have been important enough for Ruth to have taken it from Morning Breeze and for Morning Breeze to chase after her."

White Eagle, now dressed in faded jeans, a large silver belt, a jean shirt and a turquoise bolo, studied the map for a long time. He turned it on its side and then finally upside down. Then the rabbi saw a small bead of water form in his eye and drop onto the map. It was as if a piece of his soul had snapped off and turned into a mournful tear. He looked at the rabbi, his face ashen, his body shaking. In a melancholy voice he added, "Morning Breeze didn't sell his vote, he sold out our ancestors, our very spirit." He paused to take a deep breath and let out a long sigh. "Ruth had many talents and many loves. She loved history, especially the history of the Antchu people, her adopted people. She used to give tours at our museum. Many of the women who would talk to those who came would put everyone to sleep, especially the children. When Ruth talked about our history, everyone listened because her heart spoke directly to their hearts. She helped me search for old documents and maps. She was the one who learned how to read the maps, to listen to their teachings. I should have looked at this map more closely when I first gave it to you. I never had patience for maps. But now I understand."

With that, White Eagle stood up and went to the rabbi's bookshelves and, first looking to the rabbi for approval, took out three books at random. He then placed two books carefully on the rabbi's desk about a foot apart. "The first book represents the casino, the second the new council building. This third book," which he then placed next to the casino, "is an old Antchu burial site according to the map. Ruth had earlier come across old documents suggesting that there was a burial site on the reservation. It referred to an old army map. No one took her seriously. Neither did I. This is the map. She must have recognized it right off."

The rabbi stood up. "My guess is Morning Breeze let those who wanted to build the casino know he had the power to stop its construction because of the forgotten burial site unless he was paid off. He probably kept the map as his insurance policy."

Ann also stood and said, "I presume now the casino will be closed down and moved."

Blue Star spoke up, "No, they have a dilemma. Because the reservation only borders the main road for a very small area, there's no place to move the casino. There will be some who say that it is too bad the casino was built on a burial ground, but it is too late. They will suggest maybe there is a way to honor the site. Put up a memorial or something. They won't want the past to destroy their hope for the future. Others will demand the spirits of the ancestors be honored and the casino torn down."

"It seems they have the classic fight between holding on to the tradition as a lifeline or cutting loose the past to allow the future to unfold," observed the rabbi.

There was silence. White Eagle spoke up, "When I was coming in, I noticed a marker for the victims of the Holocaust. I had some time to read while in jail and I read more about your history. I am again sorry for how angry I got at you. Our people do have much in common. I wonder if you wouldn't mind saying a prayer for Ruth out at that memorial?"

The rabbi picked up a prayer book and they all walked outside. It was a sunny day and someone had put some fresh flowers at the base of the marker that spoke of so much pain and darkness.

White Eagle, Carol, Blue Star, Ann and Rabbi Daniels all stood in front of the memorial with their own thoughts. Rabbi Daniels finally spoke. "For my people, this represents an end and thus a new beginning. In a similar way, we've learned what Ruth wanted us to learn. Her soul can now rest. When someone dies, there's a Jewish tradition of *krea*, or tearing. The sound of cloth ripping, the physical release of gripping a garment and pulling, announces there is an end, a change. This is the suit I was wearing when I met White Eagle in the jail." With these words, the rabbi took hold of his lapel and ripped the suit slowly letting the sound echo off the building and bury itself in their memories. Then Rabbi Daniels recited the Kaddish prayer, the traditional memorial prayer for the dead. The rabbi could feel Leah's hand in his when he finished.

Epilogue

G-d was in this place and I did not know it.
Genesis

Sue returned to the rabbi's study. It had been a long time since she had been in his office. The roll top desk was still covered by the mountain of books and papers. She looked at the books and recalled many of their discussions. She was going to miss her regular meetings with this man who was her teacher, her rabbi.

"Well, congratulations," Rabbi Daniels boomed. "That was a beautiful conversion ceremony last week. You are now an MFT."

"What is an MFT?" asked Sue with a lilt in her voice.

"A member of the tribe." He paused for a moment. "Your speech about your new Hebrew name was most touching. I'm glad you invited White Eagle and the others."

"After all that we've gone through, I wanted to keep Ruth's name alive. And anyway, Ruth is a good name for a convert as she was the first one to become an MFT."

The rabbi changed to a more formal voice, "Well, you had your ritual immersion, your official ceremony, you've read and studied, and now there is one last thing." He took out a blue cloth bag, "On behalf of the Congregation, we present to you a prayer shawl, a *talit*. May you wear it proudly and may you feel your people's embrace of love." With that comment, he removed the beautiful blue and white shawl and wrapped it around Sue as they both said the blessing of being enwrapped by the fringes. "May you always look about these fringes as a reminder that you are to be a blessing to this world through your actions, through the *mitzvot*."

As the rabbi escorted her out of his office, Ann came out to congratulate Sue as well. They both were walking Sue to her car in the parking lot when a gruff-looking man approached. "Rabbi Daniels, I got your trailer."

"Great," exclaimed the Rabbi. He excused himself and followed the visitor. Ann chatted with Sue. Their talk was accompanied by the sound of a sledgehammer pounding on metal in the direction of the rabbi's parking space.

The rabbi returned and bid Sue farewell. Then he turned to Ann.

"You're coming with me, Ann, aren't you?" The rabbi was bubbling with enthusiasm. He had a slightly crazy glow in his eyes.

"Where're you going? You don't have time to go anywhere," asserted Ann. "You've got your class in Basic Judaism."

"No, I'm having Judy Meyer come in to teach them how to cook. Her matzo balls are famous. They won't miss me."

The two began walking towards the rabbi's car.

In front of Ann sat an Odyssey van, the rabbi's second car, which Brenda usually used to transport the kids. The rabbi's little sports car would not work for this job. The van now had a monstrous wooden flat bed trailer attached to its rear bumper.

"Is that part of your secret mission?"

"Yes."

"Count me in. This I've got to see."

A few minutes later the Odyssey was moving quickly down a dirt road, the trailer clanking along behind as though it was about to smash apart.

"I've adopted your driving style," the rabbi boasted.

"So I see," said Ann, clutching the armrest. "And so it only seems fair I adopt your terror."

Ann recognized the look in the rabbi's eyes. She'd seen it in people before. She'd seen it on her own face as well. The speed at which the rabbi drove was irrelevant; he was imbued with invincibility.

"Ann, I'm proud of some of the things I've done in my life. I'm even amazed at some. But one thing all my accomplishments have had in common was that they were guaranteed to win approval. A rabbi is well respected and so is a lawyer. Now I have something to do that isn't going to win much approval. You remember those stones at the retreat house when your car broke down?"

"How could I forget? You mention them every time we meet."

"I've decided they need to be taken home."

"Do you plan to use them for a walkway to your house?"

"No, not my home. Their home."

"And where is their home?"

"I've done research. I've talked to people, including White Eagle. Everyone believes that they were part of a Hamshu burial site. But, it can't be proven."

"You're a clever lawyer. I'm sure you can find a way."

"I did try. There is simply no way to get people to care about a bunch of rocks that look like a bunch of other rocks. I couldn't get anywhere. No one seems to really understand my obsession. But, I brought my check book and credit cards to cover our bail if we're caught."

Something flashed in Ann's mind. "Wait. This is the second time I've heard you talk about bail. What exactly am I getting myself into? Are we going to pick up those stones and move them someplace?"

"Yes!" said the rabbi. "Great, isn't it?"

"Everyone will know you took them. You could be arrested for stealing. You could even lose your license as an attorney. Maybe the university will not hire you?"

"Yes, isn't it beautiful?"

Ann looked worried. The rabbi picked up on it. "Maybe, but I don't think the synagogue will fire me over this."

"I don't understand. What do you care what the temple thinks. You've resigned."

"Well, the president asked me to think about it. And I've been thinking. I really do love helping people. And, I wouldn't have had this adventure. And, to be honest, I wouldn't have as much fun without you listening to my phone conversations. If it's okay with you, of course?"

Ann couldn't believe how happy she felt. "Rabbi, if no one else will take you and you have to stay with this crazy community, I'm in. And, if you need to do something with those rocks and it's your mission, it's your mission. Sometimes we have to do what we have to do even when no one else understands. I don't understand. But I'll help. As long as you'll pay my bail if we get arrested."

The rabbi smiled. He hummed *Eli, Eli.*

"That's the song you sang at your first sweat, isn't it."

Rabbi Daniels nodded and continued to hum for a while. "By the way, I called Matt. It was one of the hardest calls I ever made. He initially didn't want to take my call because the lawyer had told him not to talk to anyone about this. And he knows I'm an attorney and feared I would try to get him to confess. But after a few minutes we even started listening to each other. We're going to meet next week. I'm not sure what the result will be but I do feel a little freer, since if I'm not locked in that prison of hatred quite as much. I've realized I've been searching for a long time for something and that search is bringing me back to my Judaism, my community, my family, and myself."

Awhile later, the van with the trailer attached had navigated the narrow road and was parked next to the stones at the old De la Guerra retreat house.

As the rabbi got out of the van, he quipped, "Let's see what shape we are in." With that, he gave a pair of gloves to Ann and put on a pair of his own. He began lifting the stones as did Ann. It didn't take long before there were stones resting on the flat bed and two sweaty people were sitting under a tree nearby.

"Couldn't we hire someone to help?" implored Ann, rubbing her shoulder.

"We're over half of the way there. We'll make it."

"We've lifted the smallest ones. The rest are bigger," she pointed out.

"You can keep me company," he grunted, moving back to the fountain. He took off his shirt. He took out a moving pad from the trunk of his car. He laid it on the ground and rolled a heavy stone on it. He dragged it fifteen feet to the trailer and then he lifted it onto the trailer. Ann's muscle power was temporally spent. The only way she could think to help was to sing *Oseh Shalom*, a song about peace. The rabbi joined her. He felt revived. Stronger.

"Our ancestors were slaves to pharaoh and lifted stones to build the cities of Piithom and Raamses," stated the rabbi. He heaved another stone on the trailer.

"Yes, and that's why they've been dedicated to mental skills ever since," suggested Ann, now rolling a particularly round stone toward the trailer.

Two hours later, every stone was on the trailer. Ann and the rabbi sat on the ground in pain.

"I can't even raise my arm," moaned the rabbi.

"Rabbi, there's no way we can unload any of these stones. Forget it."

"Don't worry. We won't have to. I have help lined up at the other end."

When the rabbi's arm muscles returned to partial usefulness, he and Ann climbed back into the Odyssey. It groaned. It strained. It barely moved along the ground toward the dirt road.

"You think it can make it?" asked Ann.

"This van has power, I hope."

A full one hour later the van pulled the trailer up past the casino. The rabbi went down a side road and stopped. The casino was not far away, but was hidden by a hill. White Eagle was sitting on the ground. He got up and walked over to the van.

"Well, here they are," the rabbi announced, getting out of the van and motioning to the pile of rocks.

White Eagle stared at the stones without emotion. "There are many stones here."

"You brought help, didn't you?" asked the rabbi.

"Yes," he answered. White Eagle turned in the opposite direction and shouted in a raspy voice, "He's here."

Five men dressed in dirty jeans and faded plaid shirts appeared from behind some bushes where they had been resting out of the sun. "These are friends of mine."

Introductions went on for several minutes. There were strained handshakes. All the men had black hair, messy and fairly long, except for one man, whose haircut was short and clean. They all stared at the stones in the same dumbfounded way White Eagle did.

"What are they for?" one of them asked.

They're sacred," affirmed the rabbi. He was suddenly embarrassed.

There was a pause. "Stones can be very sacred," agreed White Eagle. "Where do you want them?"

The rabbi had hoped the arrival of the stones at the spot he and White Eagle had discussed was all that was necessary. He had not thought of what to do with them. Perhaps placed in a circle, a mound? He tried to drum up enthusiasm by looking around with vigor. "Well, I guess..."

White Eagle closed his eyes and groped around in the air as though he were using a water witch. "How about here?" he asked, pointing to a particular flat patch of earth. "I think they belong here."

The rabbi was encouraged by White Eagle's confidence. "Yes, I agree." The five men began picking up stones from the trailer and putting them on the ground. The rabbi picked up one too, but an arm muscle immediately began to cramp. He laid the stone back down.

"Did you gather all these by yourself?" asked White Eagle.

"Just the two of us," he answered.

"Then you sit," White Eagle. "They are strong. They can do it."

A half hour later all of the stones were off the trailer and on the ground. Three of the men left. The remaining two sat on the ground with White Eagle, Ann, and the rabbi. When a cigarette was lit, Ann got up and moved up wind. The rabbi thought of doing the same, but decided against it. No one had anything to say.

Finally, White Eagle began to chant softly, a deep guttural chant. Soon the two men began to chant with him. It was an earthy sound. A tribal intonation that sparked something in the rabbi. The rabbi reached into his pocket where he kept the *kippah* while he was carrying the stones and placed it on his head. He began to sing *El na refana la*, "Please G-d, heal her," an ancient healing prayer used by Moses to ask G-d to heal Miriam. He was asking for healing for White Eagle, Ruth's soul, and for himself.

The chanting grew loud. The rabbi's prayer became more spirited. White Eagle and his two friends were slapping their hands on their legs in rhythm, and the rabbi rocked back and forth. He felt curiously free from any sense of embarrassment.

The electrifying ritual reached a zenith, and then everyone stopped simultaneously.

A sense of bliss filled the rabbi.

The sun began its descent below the horizon, and the pre-twilight played magic on the stones. They were glowing and the veins were alive with the illusion of movement.

"These are good stones," White Eagle declared in his slow deliberate voice. "They are piled in the shape of the Anabella Mountains." He pointed out the outline of the stone pile, now distinct against the sky.

The rabbi was puzzled. "The Anabella Mountains are in the Southwest," White Eagle reminded the rabbi. "Ruth had been there many times. It was her place of peace. It was there that she decided she wanted to marry me," White Eagle continued.

"This is *bershert* - meant to be," explained the rabbi.

"Absolutely," chimed Ann.

"This will be a monument to Ruth," added White Eagle. "And to all our people who died. And to Leah, her spirit is here as well. Perhaps they can rest in peace."

The rabbi was silent, a tear escaping from one of his eyes.

White Eagle then said, "I've found a new trailer to live in on the reservation. I'm teaching again and I'm fighting for the casino to be moved. I'll probably lose, but I won't drink again. Thank you again, my brother." After a warm hug, he left with his two friends. Ann and the rabbi were alone.

"We may still get in trouble with the law," mused Rabbi Daniels.

"Yes," replied Ann.

"But it feels good, what we did, doesn't it!" emphasized the rabbi with gusto. "And I feel good!"

About the Author

Arthur Gross Schaefer wears many hats as rabbi, educator, and as a former practicing lawyer and CPA. He is an award winning university professor and department chair of business law and marketing at Loyola Marymount University. He was recently named as one of the top 300 professors in the United States by the *Princeton Review*. Rabbi Arthur, as he is called by his congregation, leads the spiritually based Community Shul of Montecito and Santa Barbara. Professor Gross Schaefer speaks and writes on professional and personal ethics, effective ethical decision-making, academic freedom, medical ethics, freedom of religion, spirituality in the workplace, burnout for attorneys, clergy and business professionals. He is also the chairman of the board for the Avi Schaefer Fund, named after his deceased son Avi and devoted to changing the campus climate around the Israeli-Palestinian debate on college campuses. His wife, Laurie Gross Schaefer, is an internationally known artist and liturgical consultant. He views his sons Elisha, Yoav, Avi z"l, and Noah as his university.

Recent Titles from Gaon Books

Mati Milstein. 2012. *My New Middle East: Inside the Israeli Conundrum.*

Michael L. Kagan. 2012. *God's Prayer.*

Raphael David Elmaleh and George Ricketts, 2012. *Jews under Moroccan Skies: Two Thousand Years of Jewish Life.*

Isabelle Medina Sandoval. 2012. *Hidden Shabbat: The Secret Lives of Crypto-Jews.*

Zalman Schachter Shalomi and Netanel Miles Yepez. 2011. *A Hidden Light: Stories and Teachings of Early HaBaD and Bratzlav Hasidism.*

Estrella Jalfón de Bentolila, 2011. *Haketía: A Memoir of Judeo-Spanish Language and Culture in Morocco.*

Sandra K. Toro, 2011. *Princes, Popes and Pirates.*

Zalman Schachter Shalomi and Michael L. Kagan. 2011. *All Breathing Life Adores Your Name.*

With the collaboration of:

Gaon Institute
A 501 c 3 organization that supports
tolerance and diversity
www.gaoninstitute.org

CPSIA information can be obtained at www.ICGtesting.com
Printed in the USA
BVOW05s1904090915

417328BV00001B/49/P